**Richard Gordon** was born in 1921. He qualified as a doctor and then went on to work as an anaesthetist at St Bartholomew's Hospital, and then as a ship's surgeon. As obituary-writer for the *British Medical Journal*, he was inspired to take up writing full time and he left medical practice in 1952 to embark on his 'Doctor' series. This proved incredibly successful and was subsequently adapted into a long-running television series.

Richard Gordon has produced numerous novels and writings all characterised by his comic tone and remarkable powers of observation. His *Great Medical Mysteries* and *Great Medical Discoveries* concern the stranger aspects of the medical profession whilst his *The Private Life of…* series takes a deeper look at individual figures within their specific medical and historical setting. Although an incredibly versatile writer, he will, however, probably always be best known for his creation of the hilarious 'Doctor' series.

# Doctor on the Job

*Richard Gordon*

HOUSE OF
STRATUS

This edition published in 2001 by House of Stratus, an imprint of Stratus Holdings plc, 24c Old Burlington Street, London, W1X 1RL, UK.

www.houseofstratus.com

Typeset, printed and bound by House of Stratus.

A catalogue record for this book is available from the British Library.

ISBN 1-84232-508-6

# 1

On a bright Monday morning in early June, Sir Lancelot Spratt, FRCS, senior surgeon of St Swithin's Hospital, stepped through the automatically parting plate-glass entrance doors of the Bertram Bunn Wing, an annex to the towering rebuilt hospital itself. The wing was named after Sir Bertram Bunn, the St Swithin's surgeon who assisted at the removal of King Edward the Seventh's appendix on his Coronation Day in 1902 and made a fortune, His Majesty having invested appendicectomy with the respectability and publicity his descendants afforded showjumping. It appropriately catered exclusively for private patients, many of them paying in the foreign currency so relished and cherished as it rang in the near-empty vaults of the Bank of England less than a mile away.

The annex was ten storeys high, its peak the penthouse suite, brand new glass and concrete gleaming like an actress' eye-tooth. Though at the edge of the City of London, it looked upon an artfully designed garden with spraying fountains, a lily pond, neatly pruned trees and vividly flowering bushes bursting from paths of snowy gravel, suggesting on sunny days the courtyard of some grassless Eastern palace. The garden was visible through the long glass wall of the entrance hall, setting an atmosphere which in his meditative moods Sir Lancelot savoured fondly. It recalled to him the *souks* of Casablanca and Fez which he had explored as a holidaymaking young doctor, the Casbah of Algiers, countless clamorous bazaars among tortuous rough-cobbled streets, inky black when stumbled upon from the blinding white sunlight of timeless North Africa. As the glass doors slid silently together again behind him that hot morning, he remembered with an inner smile the exciting twang of strange instruments, the spicy smell of never-tasted foods, the dark eyes gazing in intriguing if exasperating isolation above the yashmak.

The Bertram Bunn's lobby, like the vast entrance hall of the new St Swithin's itself, resembled those indistinguishable, interchangeable hotels which proliferate round the world for flitting businessmen, who find themselves unable to discern in which continent they have landed or even if they are still at home. The wall opposite the garden was occupied by a white plastic counter, behind which a pair of St Swithin's porters in their brown coats and a receptionist in a white nylon overall attended to the wants and worries of patients and visitors. The luxurious wing employed the same staff as the main National Health Hospital. It was simply that section of St Swithin's designated for paying customers, by some unknown Civil Servant in the Department of Health across London at the Elephant and Castle.

At the far end of the lobby was a small shop for the patients' convenience, exactly as in St Swithin's itself. But this one was crammed with objects which Sir Lancelot often eyed enviously – expensive matching sets of golf clubs, fabulously priced shotguns, jewellery, tweeds, rare and superb brands of malt whisky, stone jars of Oxford marmalade. A glittering escalator softly mumbled, lifts whisked up and down, unmemorable music unobtrusively filled the well-conditioned air. The floor was of multicoloured patterned mosaic, upon which a pair of patients' families squatted, eating an early midday meal with their fingers from a bucket.

'Sir Lancelot –'

'Ah! Good morning, Matron.' He tried to look as if he had neither noticed her nor hoped to slip past her.

'I must see you instantly,' she hissed.

The Bertram Bunn Wing had its own matron, staring at him distractedly from the half open door of her steel-and-glass office. She was small, brisk, blonde, divorced, still in her thirties, at that moment shrimp-pink with indignation. She wore a plain dark blue dress with a large silver St Swithin's crest on the bosom, a tiny starched cap perched on her curls like the lid of a vol-au-vent and a pair of crisp muslin streamers floating down her neck.

'Couldn't it wait until lunchtime?' Sir Lancelot suggested optimistically. 'I'm already late. I should have started on the Sheikh of Shatt al Shufti's double hernia twenty minutes ago.'

'It can't wait another moment,' she told him fiercely.

'The Sheikh's probably already anaesthetized,' he objected. 'He has been impressed upon me as a person of such importance to our country's economy, I feel I hardly dare keep him waiting, even unconscious.'

'Instantly,' she repeated.

'He has taken the penthouse at vast expense, so can at least expect quick service – '

'Lancelot, you are being evasive, if not cowardly.'

Sir Lancelot Spratt submissively entered her compact office.

The senior surgeon was tall and broad shouldered, chestnut haired and ruddy faced. Imagined without his beard – which few people at St Swithin's could – like many well-reared and well-nourished Englishmen he carried into middle age a resemblance of himself as a bun-faced schoolboy. Sir Lancelot's look commanded. His smile honoured. His frown terrified. He also possessed that air of effortless eupepsia essential in the successful medical man, and though admitting that he was neither the greatest of surgeons nor of scientists, agreed that he enjoyed the priceless professional asset of knowing absolutely everyone who mattered. As for the knighthood, he claimed that honours were largely a matter of finding the plastic spaceship in your portion of cornflakes.

'This is the end,' announced the matron, as she slammed the door behind him. 'I'm tendering my resignation.'

'Oh, come,' said Sir Lancelot soothingly. 'Come, come. You must be joking?'

'Some joke!' She gave a laugh like the caress of two sheets of emery paper.

'You must not take such a decision lightly. It is a grave one for all of us in the Bertie Bunn, both staff and patients – '

'Don't talk to me about patients,' she interrupted furiously.

Sir Lancelot stood stroking his beard, suppressing both an impatience to be in the operating theatre and an impulse to lay the matron across his knee to belabour her chubby bottom. He embarked upon the scene with weariness but confidence, having played it several times before. He often felt that the newly opened Bertram Bunn Wing aggravated his normal clinical duties with administrative and diplomatic ones sufficient to sink a man of less stormproof personality.

'Patients! That's why I'm resigning. This time irrevocably. One of yours, too,' she snapped accusingly. 'The one you're just going to operate on. The one who took the penthouse and the whole top two floors. The one that man at the Foreign Office keeps ringing up, to ask if he's comfy. The one with all the Rolls-Royces.' She shuddered. 'He did it on the floor.'

'Dear me,' said Sir Lancelot mildly. He suggested charitably, 'Perhaps it was an accident?'

'Accident be damned. He does it every morning.'

Sir Lancelot assumed a pained expression. 'Doesn't he ring for a bedpan? The communication system in this wing is so highly sophisticated it is of course completely unreliable. The fire brigade with their hoses always appear for cases of cardiac arrest, and that dreadful voyeuristic television engineer whenever women go into labour –'

'Bedpan!' said the matron contemptuously. 'I offered him one. With my own hands. He waved it away, quite imperiously. His interpreter explained that he could never demean himself by sitting on so ignoble a utensil.'

'He *is* the Sheikh of Shatt al Shufti, I suppose,' Sir Lancelot reflected.

'Was that meant to be a stupid joke?'

'Good grief, no.' He chuckled. 'It was perfectly inadvertent. But rather good, don't you think?'

'Have you no sense of shame?'

'My dear Matron, you must remember that the Sheikh does it like that as a matter of course in his tent, or whatever he lives in at home. A man simply comes along with a pan and a little brush, like you see after the Household Cavalry. We must surely make allowances for foreign customs? The poor denizens of the Middle East have no hospitals of their own. So anyone who feels ill and has the money flies to London. It's nearer and cheaper than New York, and the nurses are warmer-hearted. Even our own Earl's Court Angels, whose hearty femininity and spicy language I always think brings a refreshing breeze from the Australian outback to the sickbed. Harrod's is quite as good as Macy's and the television programmes are of better quality. We're inescapably in the invisible export business, Matron. Like Anne Hathaway's cottage.'

'And I'm sick to death of it. It's bad enough with their wives and concubines sleeping all over the floors like bundles of black washing. Roasting whole sheep in the garden –'

'We enjoy our barbecues –'

'But we don't eat the entire entrails and eyes. Now there's these Africans and Chinese who seem to have all the money in the world descending on us by the hundred, not to mention the French and Italians, who to my mind can be just as coarse and smell just as badly, if different. Not that I've anything in the slightest against foreigners as such.'

The matron had gone pinker, and was shaking so violently that Sir Lancelot discerned with disquiet that she was trembling on the brink of tears. Only two items in life disturbed him, a weeping pretty woman and the smell of raw onions. He knew the matron was invaluable and irreplaceable in the Bertram Bunn Wing. He also knew that she was delicate Dresden, easily cracked. He would have to apply the putty.

'My dear, dear Matron, look at it this way. Once upon a time these Arabs were only too eager to sell us their oil. Or for that matter, their sisters. I remember a remarkable number on offer one evening out in Port Said. Now they have us firmly by the petrol pumps, it's understandable they should be as beastly arrogant towards us as we used to be towards them. Isn't it the old British Empire come home to roost? If only we'd sent a gunboat to Mr Mussadiq in his pyjamas twenty-five years ago,' he sighed. 'But unfortunately Lord Palmerston is as dead as Queen Anne. And anyway the Americans would never have let us, because they thought the British Empire dreadfully naughty and told Mr Churchill to get rid of it.'

But the matron needed solace warmer than a kiss of history. 'It's such a shame, such a waste, that this lovely new wing, crammed with the very latest scientific and medical equipment, should be dragged down to the same standards as everything else in the country. After my years of dedicated nursing, it's too much.' Her voice finally shrieked past the pressure-valve of professional decorum. 'On the floor! Polished parquet!'

She laid her blonde curls against the lapel of Sir Lancelot's formal black jacket and started to cry.

Sir Lancelot patted her briskly on the back, as though burping a baby. 'I always like to remember in trying circumstances the words of St Augustine,' he imparted soothingly. '*Let nothing disturb thee, Let nothing affright thee, All passeth away, God alone will stay, Patience obtaineth all things.*'

'Oh, Lancelot! You're so cultured. Quite unlike the younger doctors.'

'I have taken to reading in bed since the death of my poor wife.'

'That must be six months now.' She dabbed her eyes with a small, plain handkerchief.

'Near on a year.'

'How time goes by. I always think that talking to some sympathetic listener about the book you are reading makes it far more interesting.'

Perceiving how the subject of conversation had made a definite change, Sir Lancelot extracted himself from the matron's arms and nearly from her office almost before she had noticed it.

'I haven't finished yet – ' She stopped him in the open doorway. 'Pip. You know, Philip Chipps. My elder sister's boy. He's up for the clinical of his surgery finals tomorrow morning.'

'I can only wish him the best of British luck.'

'Now you're being obtuse.' She resumed her previous fieriness. 'You know perfectly well it's the poor young man's last chance. You've already failed him three times. If he doesn't pass this one, he'll be thrown out of St Swithin's for good and all. You're all dreadfully unfair on him. He may appear slightly disorganized on the surface, but that comes from a father who seems more interested in his butterfly collection than his practice. Underneath, Pip is dreadfully serious and utterly dedicated to his work.'

'Possibly. But he suffers a singular disadvantage for a surgeon. He is accident-prone.'

'That's of no significance,' she dismissed the objection. 'Because once qualified he intends to become a psychiatrist. It's just like you, Lancelot. You make up your mind you dislike somebody or something, and nothing will budge your opinion. It's exactly the same about everything else in the hospital, from your cholecystograms to your coffee.'

'I can recall the exact moment when I formed the view you mention.

When discovering it was your nephew who had tucked a hose from the cold tap into my left boot while I was scrubbed up and operating.'

'That's another tragedy about poor Pip. He's so easygoing and good natured he's easily made a fool of. He was tricked into doing it by that dreadful pair Havens and Raffles – who I am utterly horrified to see are now St Swithin's housemen. They told Pip you'd ordered it to keep your feet cool.'

'Such gullibility may equip him splendidly for a career in psychiatry. But an examiner must assume the possibility, however alarming, of him practising hard-headed medicine.'

'Please see he gets through,' said the matron, slamming the door.

Sir Lancelot shook his head slowly, picking his way past the engrossed lunchers towards the lifts. Sometimes even his own ironclad personality came within danger of foundering.

# 2

'Morning, Solly,' said Sir Lancelot, passing the St Swithin's skin specialist in the doorway of the dining-room. 'I hope you're encountering no sales resistance among our customers.'

'Some of my best patients are Arabs,' Dr Cohen told him.

The medical staff dining-room in the Bertram Bunn Wing was a small, bright apartment on the first floor, overlooking the garden. It was decorated with an allegorical mural depicting Charles Hill of the British Medical Association and Nye Bevan inaugurating the National Health Service in 1948. Both were depicted as Florence Nightingales passing soothingly with their lamps along rows of agonized, frenzied casualties, and nobody could decide if these represented the suffering public or the medical profession. Sir Lancelot always ate with his back to it.

'Hello, Lancelot, what have you been up to?' asked Sir Lionel Lychfield, the Dean of St Swithin's Medical School, looking up from *The Times* as the surgeon sat next to him at one of the square tables.

'The Sheikh of Shatt al Shufti's bilateral inguinal hernia. I did his hydroceles for an encore. I was going to leave them as shock absorbers for riding his camel, but of course the fellow hasn't had a rougher ride than a Rolls-Royce for years. I hope he won't be cross. At home, he punishes thieves by lopping off their hands. And I suppose other offenders by the removal of similarly appropriate parts. I distinctly didn't like the look of his two bodyguards lurking outside the operating theatre.'

Sir Lancelot opened the glossy-covered menu. The Bertram Bunn Wing enjoyed the reputation among medical consultants as the best place to eat in London. The food came from the same kitchens as the St

Swithin's National Health patients', but its own chef toothsomely overcame the challenge of all possible physical states, religious obligations and national or personal tastes. He provided a dozen attractive diets – low calorie, low sodium, high protein, low cholesterol, diabetic, duodenal, vegetarian, kosher, Mohammedan, Cantonese, Pekinese and Indian, as well as his normal *cordon bleu*. This nourishment being heavily subsidized, the dean ate there whenever he could in preference to the St Swithin's consultants' mess. He was famous in the hospital for a purse as tight as an oyster with lockjaw.

Sir Lancelot asked the young waitress in a green ward orderly's smock for some cheese sandwiches and a glass of orange juice. The dean ordered *entrecôte garni* with extra vegetables. 'The matron's gone neurotic again, by the way,' Sir Lancelot told him.

'I do wish she were a more stable sort of female,' the dean said testily. He was short and skinny, with a pointed bald head and large round glasses beneath straight, bristly black eyebrows. These became agitated in his frequent storms of exasperation, when they always suggested to Sir Lancelot a pair of hairy caterpillars performing a love-dance. 'But of course, she *is* highly decorative, as matrons go,' the dean conceded. 'And if you're paying an absolute fortune for your penthouse, you don't want to be ushered into it by someone with the appearance and attitude of a seaside landlady during a wet August.'

'She's threatening to go again. But she won't. She had exactly the same tantrums last January. You may remember, that was when a newly admitted patient, understandably unfamiliar with such complexities of civilization as air-conditioning controls, lit a fire in the middle of his room by chopping up the furniture. She's also been on about her nephew, Chipps. I suppose if I have to fail him in surgery again tomorrow, he's for the boot?'

'Most definitely. Can't encourage idleness in the medical school. It doesn't matter whose nephews they are, even the Minister of Social Services.'

Sir Lionel Lychfield was one of St Swithin's dozen or so consultant general physicians. But as dean of the medical school, he exercised the power and high-minded severity over its students of Dr Arnold at Rugby.

'That's the trouble with the younger generation,' he went on. 'Laziness, lack of application, no sense of purpose, complete indifference to their elders, and in fact to all authority whatever. Not all of them, naturally,' he corrected himself briskly. 'Some of our young are absolutely first-class. They restore your faith in the coming generation and humanity in general. My youngest daughter Faith, for example –'

'You told me about your youngest daughter Faith at lunch last week,' Sir Lancelot interrupted.

'Young Faith! Barely eighteen years old. Already with the serious intent and the sense of vocation of a budding Florence Nightingale.' The dean nodded proudly towards the mural. 'Faith neither smokes nor drinks nor wears jeans, and devotes her life to helping the underprivileged –'

'So you were saying last week –'

'Do you know what she's been doing all this month? Living in this austere hostel under barracklike discipline down in Fulham. On a pittance – I must say, these voluntary service organizations do quite blatantly exploit the good nature of girls like Faith. She gives the full benefit of her sweet and altruistic character to the down-and-outs they collect off the Embankment and similar places. Though I suspect most of them are simply too lazy to do a decent day's work, and if I had my way would be given a pick and sent down the coalmines.'

Noticing that Sir Lancelot was staring dreamily out of the window, the dean turned back to his newspaper, giving it an irritated shake. 'God knows what the country's coming to,' he muttered. 'Everyone today seems to think he's entitled to a job for life, doing exactly the same work for steadily rising pay, even if nobody wants in the slightest what he happens to be making. Otherwise, everyone simply comes out on strike, and lives on the benefits the rest of us have to provide under this ghastly "pipsqueak" taxation. It's a wonder there aren't still factories making horseshoes and carriage-springs –'

He broke off with a noise like a rusty gate in a gale.

'What's the matter?' asked Sir Lancelot, looking alarmed.

'They've caged our fox.' Sir Lancelot seemed puzzled. 'The St Swithin's shop steward. Or our "SS man", as I preferred to describe him,' the dean added grimly. 'That little twit who represented all the trade unionists at St

Swithin's, ever since they merged into the Amalgamated Confederation of Hospital Employees, ACHE. Read that.'

He indicated the *In brief* column.

### MALE NURSE JAILED

*Arthur Pince (22), male nurse, was imprisoned for three years at the Old Bailey for indecent exposure and shoplifting. Mr Pince asked for a record number of 82 other charges to be taken into consideration.*

'They said he was the most bent shop steward in Britain,' exclaimed the dean in anguish. 'You could have used his vertebral column for a corkscrew.'

'I know nothing about this man's activities. All politics bore me, and hospital ones to distraction. From his utterances, I always thought him a seagreen incorruptible Robespierre.'

'Muddy and loaded with valuable flotsam and jetsam, more likely,' said the dean with a bitter laugh. 'These revolutionaries are all the same. Morality and misery for the masses, sybaritism for themselves. Pince was as susceptible to flattery as an infant to chicken-pox. He took bribes – or rather presents in the interests of good employer-staff relationships – with the ease and frequency of bookmakers taking bets on Derby Day. I believe he was also susceptible in the right mood to blackmail.'

'I play golf with the President of ACHE,' reflected Sir Lancelot, but the dean was too distracted to hear.

'I wish the stupid twerp had mentioned his little legal difficulties. I've several good friends among the judges. And what's a touch of indecency, when one can't walk more than half a mile about London at night without getting one's face smashed in?'

Sir Lancelot looked puzzled. 'But if I never had any dealings with this Pince person, I don't see why any other members of the medical staff should.'

'You nevertheless enjoyed the benefit. If we hadn't kept him sweet, he'd have started interfering with the hospital's private beds.' The dean embraced his surroundings with a quick glance. 'That doesn't seem to worry you?'

'Not particularly.'

'But surely you must be in favour of private practice?' the dean asked impatiently.

Sir Lancelot sat back to meditate on this question. 'In principle, yes. I think people should be allowed to pay, to avoid dying among people they would not usually be seen dead with. Also to perform their bodily functions in solitude and switch off the television when they feel like it. And doubtless we must condone the snobbery of the Shires, by keeping their daughters from aborting in public beds. It also occurs to me that private beds could richly subsidize the free ones. But raising the standards of the lowest towards the highest, instead of vice versa, would go against the cherished principles of the British people.'

Ignoring the lecture, the dean stared resentfully at the news item. 'We shan't have the luck to be landed again in the power of an immature youth who combines sex and kleptomania. Those union bosses knew perfectly well that something fishy was going on at St Swithin's. They'll see our members of ACHE elect a really tough egg as the new SS man.'

'I deplore hospitals becoming a circus for trade union power politics, like every other institution in the country,' observed Sir Lancelot loftily, as his lunch arrived. 'But that is a trivial activity, compared with getting the patients on their feet. How unappreciated are the minor miracles of modern science,' he remarked, holding up his glass. 'This fresh orange juice is transported in little drums in a state of unrelenting iciness from the steamy groves of Florida, *Dipping through the Tropics by the palmgreen shores,* as Masefield put it, just to satisfy my passing whim in the shadow of St Paul's Cathedral. Wonderful. Sir Bertram Bunn himself could never have foreseen it.'

The dean shot him a narrow glance. Everyone at St Swithin's was saying how Sir Lancelot had mellowed since his wife died. He wondered if it was really softening of the brain.

# 3

Sir Lancelot Spratt finished his sandwiches, glanced at his watch and excused himself to the dean. He had to see a new patient.

As he stepped from the escalator which led to the ground floor, he saw that she had already arrived. The pair of brown-coated porters and the girl in the white overall behind the plastic desk were grinning and nudging each other and whispering animatedly, 'It's Brenda Bristols, just look.'

Brenda Bristols was not a great actress who could awe her public. She had instead the valuable knack of making everyone feel that one of their girl friends had stepped on to the stage or screen and was fooling about. She was immensely popular. Her *Up Your* — series of films was apparently unending. And she was unlike so many of her contemporaries, who offstage lounged about in frayed jeans and a crumpled T-shirt, looking as if they had been obliged to extract themselves hurriedly from a blazing bedroom. Brenda Bristols invoked the disciplined traditions of the 1930s, when film stars dressed to colour the drab lives of a depressed world. She had appeared in the Bertram Bunn Wing wearing a scarlet straw hat three feet across, and a long dress of green sequins cut in the front, Sir Lancelot noticed, well below the xiphisternum.

'Yo ho, Lancelot!' She waved at him, clutched him and kissed him. 'This tit of mine's all right, really?' she asked anxiously.

'An entirely benign fibroma, I assure you, my dear,' he comforted her courteously. 'A lump of no unpleasant significance whatever. I shall have it out as easily as pulling a plum from a pudding. A couple of days and you'll be home again, as right as rain.'

'People keep catching their fingers on it.' Brenda Bristols looked round the lobby. 'What a weird place. It looks like a remake of *Up Your Arabian Nights.*'

'We're very cosmopolitan here. In the sun-baked villages where these people usually partake of their lunch, they would be equally disturbed by our demanding the paraphernalia of tables, chairs, knives, forks and cruet.'

'Have you no British patients *at all*?'

'Regrettably few can afford the prices these days.'

'What happens if some poor little man gets run over outside the front door?'

'He's taken round the corner to the National Health wards of St Swithin's. They are considerably more comfortable since my days as a house-surgeon, but of course definitely package-tour compared to first class.' The corner of Sir Lancelot's eye caught the matron darting from her office by the front entrance. 'This is the famous Miss Brenda Bristols,' he introduced her. 'She's with us for a day or two. Excision of mammary fibroadenoma. My patient.'

'Go on, love, I'm more than just your patient,' said the actress playfully, fluttering eyelashes which the matron thought resembled spiders' legs. 'Sir Lancelot and I are old mates, Nurse.'

'Matron,' she corrected, in a voice like a snapping icicle.

Brenda Bristols held her gaze for a second. 'How stupid of me. Of course, you're obviously far senior to all these young nurses everywhere.'

The matron clicked her fingers towards the white plastic counter. 'A hospital porter will see you to your room. I have more important duties to perform.'

'My house-surgeon will shortly be along to examine you, Brenda. Mr Havens – you'll find him a charming young man.'

'I go for charming young men. But I thought they went out with the haircut?'

'There's colour television, two channels and one in Arabic if you're interested,' Sir Lancelot informed her helpfully. 'And the *pâtisseries* at teatime I understand to be exquisite.'

'I wasn't aware that you were even acquainted with this...this comedienne,' said the matron sharply, as Brenda Bristols was escorted zealously by both porters to the lifts.

'We have a common interest in the drama. I have become a regular theatregoer since the death of my wife.'

The matron synchronously clasped her hands and pursed her lips. 'I hope you remember your Hippocratic Oath?'

'I don't think I've ever read it. It never seems to be written down anywhere, only bits of it carved over medical school doorways.'

'You should have sent her to one of the other St Swithin's consultants. Surely you fully realize the danger of a surgeon mixing his professional and personal attentions?'

'I am past the age when I did not realize it fully,' he told her severely. 'And then I always disregarded it, anyway. But I am hardly one of the trendy young practitioners who would wish the General Medical Council so to attenuate our ethical code that any young woman might literally find herself in bed under the doctor.'

'I'm sorry, Lancelot,' she apologized, suddenly meek. 'You know how upset I am today. I'm not going to resign after all. I'm a dedicated nurse. So I shouldn't be put out in the slightest if my patients do anything anywhere.'

Sir Lancelot was not able to offer his congratulations on her wise redecision, nor even his commendation of such professional stoicism. At that moment, a small, round, well-scrubbed looking man in a grey business suit and thick-rimmed glasses appeared through the sliding plate-glass doors. 'Freddie, I am delighted to welcome you in person to the Bertram Bunn Wing,' Sir Lancelot greeted him.

'Have I come to the right door?'

'Not exactly. This is Lord Hopcroft, Matron, Chairman of Hopcroft Hotels,' Sir Lancelot introduced him. 'He is said to be responsible for more sleepers than British Rail.'

'Not these hard times, I'm afraid,' said Lord Hopcroft with a woebegone look. 'Some of my more expensive hotels are as quiet as Sleeping Beauty's palace.'

'I recommended Lord Hopcroft to come for a routine check-up, now that our quite amazing new diagnostic system is installed.'

'It won't take long, will it?' he asked worriedly. 'As usual, I'm horribly busy. Can I tell my chauffeur to wait?'

'By all means. It will take no time at all,' Sir Lancelot assured him. 'Everything is completely computerized. I don't really understand these machines. Do you, Matron?'

'Thoroughly, Sir Lancelot. I have been on a course.'

'I gather it sorts out any possible physical defects electronically, in a flash. To my mind, its main advantage is not facing the patient with a series of po-faced doctors asking how much he drinks and why doesn't he lose weight. It apparently thinks a million times faster than we old-fashioned human surgeons, who need half a day to explore every bodily avenue and be sure we've left no gallstone unturned.'

'I'm certainly a strong advocate of electronic aids to efficiency,' Lord Hopcroft said firmly. 'Computers may attract a number of witless jokes, but our modern world could never run without them. In my office, we can tell you instantly the credit rating of millions and millions of British people. And they don't even know the information has been chalked up,' he declared proudly. 'I'll just nip out, and tell my chauffeur to hang about.'

As Lord Hopcroft stepped out of the sliding doors, two other visitors stepped in. One was a large African, in a bright blue suit and a broad tie with red and yellow lightning flashes on it. He was fat, glistening, many chinned, with an expression of bubbling jollity. His companion looked to Sir Lancelot an Indian, small, thin, threadbare, greyish-complexioned and miserable.

'The great Sir Lancelot?' exclaimed the fat man at once, advancing into the lobby and extending a plump hand enthusiastically. 'It sure is a big pleasure. I bring respected and feeling greetings from our revered President and Minister of Health, the great and glorious Field Marshal himself.'

'You must be Professor Ding?' Sir Lancelot remembered. 'From Shanka?'

'Correct one hundred per cent, Sir Lancelot,' the professor returned delightedly. 'I asked your name at the great St Swithin's Hospital, and they say to come round here. I'm sure glad to meet you, Sir Lancelot, particularly as we're in the same line of business.'

'And your friend – ' Sir Lancelot politely held out his hand.

Professor Ding laughed uproariously for some seconds, tears squeezing from his closed eyes. 'That sure is the funniest thing what you just said,' he managed to articulate at last. 'That is no friend. That is my patient.'

'I see.' Sir Lancelot turned to the matron. 'Professor Ding has come to St Swithin's under a special international arrangement, to perform the first heart transplant in Shankian history.'

'I sure am. Our great President and Minister of Health, he mighty proud of the fact. He say, "You go to St Swithin's, boy, the well known and learned London hospital, they got all the facilities for this sort of stuff, you swap a few hearts just to get the feel of the thing, then you come home and swap hearts right here in Shanka, just to your heart's content."' Professor Ding roared again. 'Heart's content! I made a joke. Heart's content! Get it?'

'Very droll,' said Sir Lancelot.

'All I waiting for now is one of you Britishers have a slight accident with a bus, or maybe a taxi would do, then you haul him into the famous St Swithin's Hospital, and say, "By Jimminie, he's a croaker!" Then you hook him up to the wunnerful breathing machine and keep him going off the electric mains till I got time to open up my patient here. And I slip one heart out and slip another one in, easy as changing my shoes.'

'You've had considerable experience of heart surgery in Shanka, I take it?' Sir Lancelot asked.

'Oh, sure. Them slobs out there queuing up for heart operations. Our great Minister of Health, he organize that. Besides, I read all Christiaan Barnard's book, all the way through.'

'May I ask what precisely is the diagnosis?' inquired Sir Lancelot, glancing at the patient, who seemed to have become greyer during the conversation.

'Diagnosis?' Professor Ding looked puzzled. 'Oh, sure…he got the tetrology of Fallot. In fact, the cardiac works.'

'Fallot's tetrology is certainly a serious quadruple of congenital cardiac defects,' observed Sir Lancelot, stroking his beard. 'But surely, it usually comes to notice immediately at birth? And its unfortunate sufferers seldom reach adult life?'

'He a case of arrested development, maybe?' Professor Ding laughed again, slapping his patient hard on the back. 'Well, we gotta be getting along, take a look round the town, maybe see the famous Marks and Spencers. We gotta get it all in while we can, hey?' he demanded jovially of his companion. 'This very minute, some poor Britisher maybe try looking up the underside of them lovely big red buses, then it's coats off and sleeves up and get stuck in there digging.' He clapped Sir Lancelot on the shoulder, grabbed his patient by the biceps, and hurried back to the sunlight.

'The professor seems a jolly fellow,' Sir Lancelot observed.

'That patient doesn't look remotely like one with a Fallot's tetrology,' the matron declared.

'It may be some lesser cardiac defect. All professors tend to exaggerate. I suppose it's an enormous prestige symbol for Shanka, having its own cardiac transplant. All the smaller countries have been eager getting into the act, including our own. They used to be contented with simply sporting their own national airline.'

'Which was probably less lethal.'

Sir Lancelot nodded. 'I can never entirely disagree with the definition of cardiac transplantation as the only operation which kills two patients at once.'

'Where *is* Shanka?' asked the matron, frowning.

'Search me. These African states seem to change names and regimes with bewildering speed. One day we shall wake up to find the Republic of South Africa become New Zululand or some such. The new rulers will pass a law saying "For black, read white", and I suppose their exclusively black teams will face hostile anti-apartheid demonstrations whenever they appear at Lord's or Twickenham.'

Lord Hopcroft reappeared with a businesslike step, after instructing his chauffeur to wait. Sir Lancelot apologized that he had a clinic in St Swithin's itself. 'Matron will make you quite at home,' he assured the patient, departing. 'She and the computer share a certain empathy.'

The matron led Lord Hopcroft across the lobby and through a small door in the corner beside the lifts. Together they walked down a narrow, whitepainted, empty, echoing corridor. The piped music was silent. The air-conditioning was several degrees lower. Lord Hopcroft could not fend off an intrusion of uneasiness.

The corridor ended in a plain door marked CID.

'What's this?' he asked sharply.

'The Clinical Investigation Department, of course,' the matron told him, he thought disdainfully.

They entered a small, white room, starkly lit by fluorescent tubes. He noticed they gave her a bluish, corpselike complexion. In the centre stood a transparent plastic capsule, containing a plastic stool and a stand supporting a television screen.

'That is the diagnostic box,' the matron indicated. 'Please do not approach until the red light flashes above the screen. Beneath it you will find three buttons, marked "Yes", "No", and "Uncertain". You answer the questions which appear on the screen by pressing the appropriate one."

'But supposing I should make a mistake?' Lord Hopcroft asked, surprised at the anxiety in his voice. 'I mean, it would be quite feasible, like misdialling on the telephone.'

'Please try not to. But all mistakes are automatically rejected, once the computer has created a model of your clinical profile. It will simply order you to return and repeat the test.'

'But supposing *it* makes a mistake?'

'The computer does not make mistakes. It is impossible.'

'Then what happens next?'

'According to your clinical profile, the computer will tell you to proceed through one of the two doors opposite.'

The patient had not noticed them. They were hardly distinguishable from the white wall, one marked IN the other OUT.

' "Out" leads directly to the street,' the matron informed him. "In" leads to the next stage of diagnostic investigation, if thought necessary.'

'Thought necessary by whom?'

'By the computer.'

'But doesn't Sir Lancelot have a say in things somewhere?' he asked uneasily.

'Human agency is unable to interfere with the computer. There is some iced water in the corner. Good afternoon.'

She left him. The door which clicked shut was handleless and almost invisible in the wall. 'It's a sort of medical dungeon,' he muttered. He looked round nervously. 'It all helps you to concentrate, I suppose.' With both hands he tugged down the ends of his grey jacket. 'What am I worrying about? Me, an important man, described in the newspapers as "Baron Bed-and-breakfast"? I've never had a day's illness in my life, play two rounds of golf a week, don't smoke, hardly drink, feel as fit as a flea – ' He jumped as the red light flashed, accompanied by a loud intermittent buzzing.

Lord Hopcroft squeezed through a gap in the plastic dome. Instantly the flashing and buzzing ceased. He sat on the stool. Nothing happened. He drummed his fingers lightly on the screen and whistled a soft tune. He began to wonder if something had fused. The blank screen suffused a bright blue. A question appeared in silvery capitals.

ARE YOUR PERIODS REGULAR?

Lord Hopcroft scratched his head. He wondered for a moment if it referred to some mannerism of speaking. He decided it best to do nothing. After a minute the silvery question flashed several times, to be replaced with,

ANSWER!

He pressed 'Uncertain'. The letters flicked away at once, replaced with,

ARE YOU ON THE CONTRACEPTIVE PILL?

He replied promptly, 'No'. The next question asked,

DID IT ITCH?

After some deliberation, he pressed 'No' again.

DO YOU GET THESE URGES OFTEN?

'Matron!' cried Lord Hopcroft.

Only the echoes sounded in his ears. The question started flashing. In exasperation he pressed 'Yes'. He was asked in quick succession DO YOU GET UP AT NIGHT TO URINATE?, to which he said 'No', MANY TIMES?, to which he replied 'No' again, and MORE OR LESS THAN A DOZEN TIMES?, to which he bad-temperedly slammed all three buttons at once. GO THROUGH 'IN' DOOR IMMEDIATELY, commanded the screen, then went blank.

Lord Hopcroft had the impression of some fault creeping into the system. But he obediently quit the capsule and pushed open the door marked IN. Like most patients, he clutched a faith in his hospital and his doctors which was infinite, touching and potentially disastrous.

The further room was similar but even more frightening. The signal above another television screen was already flashing and buzzing amid a scientific jungle of apparatus, all glittering metal and glass.

PASS A SPECIMEN INTO THE YELLOW FUNNEL,

the screen was ordering him.

In his agitated mental state, Lord Hopcroft found this difficult. The message flashed, to be succeeded with,

'PLEASE TRY.'

No luck.

YOU *MUST* PROVIDE A SPECIMEN, the screen exhorted. THINK OF NIAGARA FALLS.

'You bloody stupid thing,' Lord Hopcroft cried angrily.

KEEP CALM! it replied.

'I utterly refuse to keep calm. If you must know, I've been secretly fed up with you computers for years. You've come to completely dominate our lives. You're fickle, unreliable, and seldom give a straight answer. You refuse to accept the slightest criticism, and you overreact wildly at any attempt to correct your glaring faults. In fact, you're exactly like women. And a damn sight more expensive to keep. Once I'm back in my office, I'm going to loose my computers into the street, and issue my staff with ledgers bound in lovely leather and quill pens.'

ABUSE WILL GET YOU NOWHERE, it told him.

'Yes, it will.' He seized the screen furiously and tried to shake it, but it was rigidly anchored to the desk. 'Furthermore, you seem to imagine I've got a bladder like a camel.'

TAKE YOUR HANDS OFF ME!

'You're lucky I don't smash your screen in.'

YOU WOULDN'T DARE.

'Yes, I would. You just see.'

VIOLENCE IS DESPICABLE.

'So is gross incompetence.'

PLENTY OF OTHERS APPRECIATE ME.

'Plenty of others appreciated Fanny Hill.'

NOW NOW!

'Matron!' Lord Hopcroft's voice rang out plaintively. 'I want to go home. Let me out.'

His only answer was the screen flashing,

PASS A SPECIMEN INTO THE YELLOW FUNNEL.

Lord Hopcroft stared round. He saw a second stand of iced water. He filled several plastic beakers and tipped them down the funnel, laughing wildly. The whole screen flashed several times. It said,

YOU MUST ENTER HOSPITAL AT ONCE.

'Nonsense,' said Lord Hopcroft.

The door behind him flew open, and two large men in high-necked white jackets seized him by the arms and carried him out.

# 4

Shortly after eight o'clock the following morning, at the workaday end of Chelsea's King's Road, where the boutiques and bistros give way to the football ground and the gasworks, a first-floor window shot up and a pale, good-looking, wild-haired young man in a frilled shirt and velvet dinner-jacket stuck his head through the curtains and remarked, 'My God, it's daylight.'

He ducked back into the small room, staring at his wristwatch. He shook it and tapped it. A long struggle to keep up with swift-footed time seemed finally to have killed it. The softly-ticking bedside clock caught his attention. 'My God,' he said again. 'And it's Tuesday.'

He stared round, wondering where his trousers were. The floor was plastic tiled, bare except for a bra, black tights, a crumpled dress. The bed was plain and narrow, jammed into the walls like a ship's bunk. Half-covered by a sheet, long fair hair delicately curtaining her naked shoulders, both hands tucked under one glowing cheek, Faith Lychfield lay peacefully asleep.

The young man gingerly touched her nose with the tips of his fingers. She remained exactly as she was, but her eyes opened instantly, as if by some reflex.

'Hello,' she said.

'Remember me?' he asked politely.

'Of course. Wasn't it a super party?'

'It was great, terrific. And I thought it was going to be deadly boring. I mean, the Annual Ball of the Destitute Reclamation Society doesn't sound extra swinging, does it? I only went along because somebody gave me a ticket. I thought it would at least take my mind off my work.'

'It's all a frightful charity swindle, really. I can't see how the destitutes get much, once they've paid for all the champers.'

'But of course, I never wildly imagined I'd ever meet anyone so tremendously exciting and so vibrant as you there,' he told her in a sober tone, sitting demurely on the edge of the bunk in his shirt-tails.

'You *are* sweet,' she said, still in the same position.

'I must have dropped off to sleep,' he suggested lamely.

'It was awfully late when we climbed in through that window. Almost dawn. It's a wonder we weren't arrested. Policemen seem to be so suspicious these days.'

'But how do I get out? This is a woman's hostel, isn't it?'

'Don't worry. The old ducks in charge are tremendously free and easy. They have to be, or they wouldn't get any voluntary helpers. Of course, my parents think it's a cross between Holloway and a nunnery. Daddy has rather old-fashioned ideas.'

'Daddy,' he murmured, scratching his bristly chin. 'It could be just a little awkward, you know.'

'But, lovey! Daddy never need know you'd been here. Or that you'd ever met me. He keeps me away from the students as though they were lepers with bells.'

'Yes, but I ought to be seeing daddy in – ' He shook his watch, put it to his ear, then remembered the bedside clock. 'Thirty-eight minutes. I'm taking my surgery clinical in St Swithin's at nine.'

Faith sat bolt upright, hand to mouth. 'Oh, Pip! You should have told me. I'd have set the alarm.'

'The thought did pass through my mind. But I felt it would sound a rather prosaic suggestion in the circumstances.'

'You'll have to rush like the wind,' she urged. 'Daddy can be absolutely tigerish with people who don't keep appointments.'

'Yes, I'll get a move on,' he decided gravely. 'But where are my trousers?'

'Oh, dear, dear…' Faith gazed round her cubicle, lit by a bar of sunlight evading the drawn curtains. 'Did you take them off in here?'

'It might have been outside,' he admitted. 'I remember we were in rather a hurry.'

'Here they are!' She tugged a crumpled pair of dark trousers from the bottom of her bed.

'Thank you.' He started putting them on. 'I don't honestly think it's worth looking for my bow tie.'

'But you *are* at least going to *try* taking the exam, surely?' she asked with concern.

'I shall have to.' He gave a slight shrug. 'Otherwise daddy will throw me out.'

'Oh, no! You should have told me, Pip. I never imagined that you lived a life so desperate. I would have packed you back to your landlady for a cup of Ovaltine and a good night's sleep,' she told him firmly.

'I would allow myself to be thrown out of far better places than St Swithin's for last night,' he assured her solemnly.

She put her head on one side. 'What's your other name?'

'Chipps.'

'I don't know anything about you. Except that I remember daddy mentioning your name now and then at home. It always seemed to make him rather excited.'

'My own father's a GP in the West Country. He was a student at St Swithin's with yours. My mother writes poetry, which is published in the local paper. My auntie is matron of the Bertie Bunn Wing.'

'Who's trying to make Sir Lancelot Spratt,' Faith said brightly. 'Everybody knows.'

Pip winced. 'Sir Lancelot Spratt. I shall be looking him in the face –' He took another glance at the clock. 'In thirty-six minutes.'

'You *will* have to shift a bit,' she remarked, still sitting in bed.

'I'll get there. Don't worry. Even if I have to steal a car. I really mustn't fail this time. I think it would give my poor father a coronary. It's my third try at the surgery, you see. And dad's dreadfully keen that I should follow him as another doctor from St Swithin's. May I see you again tonight?'

'Of course.' She pouted her lips for him to kiss briefly.

'We have so many ideas in common.'

'Yes.' Her eyes shone into his. 'The freedom of the individual –'

'No police,' he agreed with a nod. 'No bosses. No landlords. No exams. No elite.'

'Squatters' rights – '

'Housing on demand. Plus essential foodstuffs, transport, holidays and abortion.'

'No cruel sports. Flog all huntsmen.'

'Abolish the Army and the Navy. Also Ascot Week.'

They looked at each other, almost breathless with their reforming zeal.

'See you at six?' he asked.

'That pub opposite Chelsea Town Hall.'

'Lovely. Where's my shoes?'

'In the bookcase.'

He slipped them on. 'I think that's everything.'

'Good luck for your clinical.'

'It'll be all right. I'm sure it will. I've never been so inspired before an examination in my life.'

Faith blew him a kiss and he nudged through the door. Then she yawned, put her head on the pillow and shut her eyes. She had the day off, and saw no reason for such adventures to mar a morning's lie-in. She had an intensely practical outlook, like her father.

Unfortunately for his chosen career, Pip did not enjoy Faith's talent for self-organization. This had rendered his admittance to the St Swithin's Medical School a mystery, which deepened in the eyes of its consultants with every year that he somehow managed to remain in it. They started ascribing it to some unspeakable secret of the dean's, remembered by Pip's father from their student days together. The dean was even growing to wish that this was true.

Pip stood on the kerb in the King's Road, blinking painfully in the strong sunlight. He dissected his problem in an unusually deliberative way. Bus or Tube would never get him across London in time. His next decision was to lie groaning in the roadway until someone summoned an ambulance. But he reflected that would whisk him only into the casualty department of a more convenient hospital, where he knew from experience he would have trouble extracting himself for several hours. A police car might prove unco-operative. He would have to hail a taxi, normally a gesture of unthinkable extravagance for a medical student on his own. As he climbed inside, he remembered that he had no money.

Shortly before five to nine, a pair of young men in white coats were anxiously pacing the wide, marble-walled, notice-bespangled entrance hall of St Swithin's Hospital. The concourse was as usual crowded with people waiting, visiting or lost, either sitting, standing or being propelled horizontally, the mass cleaved by briskly trotting nurses, ambling brown-coated porters, and doctors of all ages and degrees of importance but all with the look of being required vitally elsewhere.

'He isn't in the canteen having a quick coffee?' asked Tony Havens. Sir Lancelot Spratt's house-surgeon was burly, dark-haired, clean shaven and wearing at that moment an unaccustomed frown of intense concern.

'He's not having anything. I've even been through the loos.' His companion was Hugo Raffles, fair, slim and pink-cheeked, one of the junior anaesthetists resident in the hospital.

'I've phoned his digs. The landlady says he hasn't been in all night. Stroppy she was, too. Got him eggs and bacon for a specially fortifying breakfast. He hasn't kipped down across in the residents' quarters, I suppose?'

'I've looked there, too. In and under every bed. We'd have surely heard by now if he'd decided to doss in the nurses' home.'

'I suppose he hasn't taken an overdose of barbiturate, to avoid facing the examiners?'

'That's most unlikely. He can never even remember what the normal dose is.'

'I'm fed up with nursing this case of chronic infantilism. Remember how we just got him here last time? When he thought the examination was the following day.'

'Which he explained to Sir Lancelot –'

'Who congratulated him on anticipating to learn the entire subject of surgery overnight. You should never give Sir Lancelot half a chance for a nasty crack. It's fatal.'

'Remember when he failed his anatomy?' Hugo reminisced.

'After being shown a pelvis, and asked to identify Alcock's canal –'

'And pointing to the vagina.'

'There he is!' Tony exclaimed.

Pip came hurrying through the front door, open frilly shirt flapping.

'What a bit of luck, running into you,' he remarked. 'Lend me a few quid.'

'If that's your only worry – ' Tony began crossly.

'I've got a taxi waiting to be paid outside. I spent all I'd got on tombola tickets.'

'Compulsive gambler, eh?' murmured Hugo.

'Do you realize, you git, that you have precisely six minutes before appearing for your surgery clinical?'

'I rather thought the time was getting on. My watch has been somewhat disrhythmic recently. But there's no need to panic. I made it in the end, didn't I?' he ended smugly.

'But you can't walk into an exam looking like that,' Tony told him sharply.

Pip stared down at his dishevelled clothes. 'I suppose I can't. But you can lend me your white coat.'

'You also need a tie.'

'And a shave,' said Hugo. 'You know how dangerous it is, giving Sir Lancelot half a chance of referring to Sweeney Todd.'

Pip rubbed his chin again. 'Perhaps I do. Well, I know I can rely on friends like you to sort me out.'

'Come on, let's at least get near the field of battle,' Tony exhorted, grabbing Pip by the sleeve of his velvet jacket.

The examination was being held in Virtue Ward, Sir Lancelot Spratt's men's surgical on the tenth floor. Surgery itself had been transformed since the heyday of Sir Frederick Treves and Sir Bertram Bunn. The surgery finals had hardly changed at all. Cases from the wards and from out-patients, whose diseases did not proclaim themselves too subtly, were invited to pit their ills against the wits of the students. The patients' fee was small, but many volunteered readily to return to the hospital for the chance of so painlessly helping to advance surgical science. Besides, the uninhibited discussion of each other's ailments during the breaks for tea and biscuits had the flattering effect of membership to an exclusive club.

The three took the lift to the tenth floor. Hugo remembered a large cupboard outside the ward, used as a store for patients' clothes and belongings. They dodged inside. Tony and Hugo had two minutes to prepare Pip, physically and mentally.

'Remember, Sir Lancelot has mellowed recently. Everyone says so. There's no need to be scared of him any more.' Tony Havens was hastily knotting round the neck of Pip's frilly shirt a pink and silver St Swithin's Cricket Club tie, with a motif of crossed bats and scalpels. 'He won't eat you.'

'Not in one bite anyway,' said Hugo Raffles, busy on Pip's chin with an electric razor.

'Yes, but do you know any of the patients?' Pip asked impatiently.

'Only two. Sir Lancelot's been switching them around this time. He knows there're too many of the old chronics who come up for exam after exam, which we all get wise to. Look out for the patient with a large lump on the back of his neck. It's a lipoma.'

'A simple lipoma should be easy enough to diagnose.' Pip nodded with gratification.

'Watch it. Don't forget to whip back the bedclothes. He's got no legs,' Tony informed him.

'I hope this shave is quite comfortable?' inquired Hugo. 'The razor's a bit ropey. It's the one they use for the ward preops.'

'Miss the absence of legs,' Tony continued severely, 'and Sir Lancelot's got you spit-roasted for not obeying the basic rule of examining the whole patient. There's one old boy you must particularly look out for. I heard he was there from last week's candidates. He's one of Sir Lancelot's old patients, a gloomy-looking skinny fellow with smooth grey hair and a camel-coloured dressing-gown. He's generally reading the *Daily Mirror*. You'd think there was nothing wrong with him, except for slight varicose veins in the left leg, which don't require treatment – '

'He's one of those trick examination cases?' Pip interrupted brightly. 'With nothing whatever the matter, but the students make up the most fantastic diagnoses – '

'Not on your life. He's got a glass eye. Miss it and you're sunk.'

'Sir Lancelot has a spectacular way of failing students with that one,' Hugo added, shaving Pip's upper lip. He takes a pencil and simply taps the glass eye smartly with the butt of it.'

'Grey-haired old boy? Camel-coloured dressing-gown? *Daily Mirror*? I'll remember that one.'

'The rest will be the usual surgical slag of bumps and bones,' Tony told him. 'I haven't been able to lay hands on any more dead certs, though I heard the rumour of a Chinaman with jaundice just to fox everybody.'

'I'm quite sure I can pass by my own unaided efforts,' Pip declared proudly. 'I feel superbly confident this morning.'

'Where did you get to all last night, anyway?' Hugo asked.

'I was at a home for destitutes.'

'Is there any room? Your breath reeks of stale booze.'

'It's champagne,' Pip told Hugo, sounding offended.

'I'd still advise you to answer all the questions out of the side of your mouth.'

The ting of a bell came from outside.

'You look good enough to kiss,' added Hugo admiringly, switching off the razor.

Pip slipped Mike's white coat over his velvet jacket. To their calls of 'Good luck!' he shot through the swing doors of the ward. Standing immediately inside was Sir Lancelot.

'Cold?' the surgeon greeted him.

'No, sir. If I'm shivering, it must be from fright.'

'Then turn down the collar of your white coat. Good God, boy,' he exclaimed, as Pip obliged. 'I thought that sort of shirt went out with Beau Brummell.'

'It has come back, sir.'

'This is an examination, not a dress show, I suppose,' Sir Lancelot admitted wearily. 'I have become so resigned to the sartorial vagaries of our students, I should not be unduly disturbed if they appeared for their finals in an ermine jock-strap and a straw hat. Of either sex.'

Pip's confidence rose. His two friends had been right. Sir Lancelot *was* mellowing. Pip had been studying energetically if disorganizedly the past six months. He felt that, barring some outrageous howler, he had a good chance of leaving the ward virtually a qualified doctor.

'I didn't know you played cricket?' added Sir Lancelot with a frown.

'I thought this tie went rather prettily with the shirt, sir.'

'H'm. Well, you can open the bowling, Mr Chipps, by taking a look at that grey-haired gentleman just over there. The one in the camel-coloured dressing-gown who's reading the *Daily Mirror*.'

What luck! thought Pip. He was already on the path to qualification. He decided to make the most of his foreknowledge. 'I think I can make at least one diagnosis in that case from here, sir.'

'Indeed?' said Sir Lancelot with interest.

Nonchalantly strolling up to his patient, Pip took a skin-pencil from the top pocket of Tony's white coat, and grasping the patient firmly by the top of the head thrust the end without a word firmly into his right eye.

'Yahhhhhhhhhhhhhhhh!' said the patient. 'You bloody maniac! Do you want to blind me?'

'Get out of the ward this instant, you juvenile Oedipus,' roared Sir Lancelot.

'Oh, bother,' murmured Pip. 'Wrong eye.'

'My dear Alfred, I do apologize,' continued Sir Lancelot hastily to the patient. 'I'm afraid there's always the risk of some student becoming completely unbalanced through the stress of the examination –'

'Unbalanced?' demanded the man in the camel dressing-gown, hopping about and clutching his eye. 'He's not unbalanced. He's a sadist. He'd commit grievous bodily harm easier than kiss my –'

'Ah, Sister, an ophthalmic dressing, quickly,' Sir Lancelot ordered, as she hurried to investigate the disturbance. 'Please let me see the injured organ,' he added with pressing solicitude, peering into the man's face. 'No permanent damage, I hope, as far as I can tell.'

'I really am most dreadfully sorry,' apologized Pip.

'Get *out*,' repeated Sir Lancelot furiously.

'Does that mean I've failed?' he inquired.

'What on earth's going on?' asked the dean, fussing into the ward wearing his white coat. 'Is one of the patients having a fit?'

'This menace to society came into the examination room and promptly started attacking people with a sharp instrument,' Sir Lancelot explained.

The dean gave his thin smile. 'Sounds like a typical surgeon.'

'This is no time for joking,' Sir Lancelot reminded him fiercely. 'The fool might well have injured the patient's one good eye for life. Worse still, he could have laid the hospital open to astronomical damages.'

This took the smile from the dean's lips. 'Exactly. It's bad enough already, patients queueing up to sue us if they so much as get a splinter under their nail from the ward draughts' board. We have to carry more insurance than a jumbo jet. Particularly as the judges are utterly reckless throwing about our money. They take a mischievous delight in getting the better of we doctors. Lose your sense of smell and you can go off on a world cruise, lose an arm and you can retire in comfort for life. We're a source of huge and unexpected wealth for the British public, like the football pools – It's you, Chipps. As I might have expected,' he recalled.

'The idiot luckily missed the cornea,' said Sir Lancelot, peering again. 'But it'll have to be bandaged up for the best part of a fortnight, I'm afraid, leaving you completely in the dark, Dimchurch. It's particularly unfortunate, as you so kindly volunteered your services out of admiration for our noble profession.'

'It is a blessing for humanity as a whole,' the dean comforted the patient. 'I can assure you that this young man, purely as a medical student, was a greater danger to the public than a berserk abattoir attendant. Had he gone into the world as a qualified doctor, he would have made the Black Death look like a flu epidemic. You should join the roll of great medical martyrs –'

'I don't want to be a bleeding martyr. I was planning to play golf this evening.'

'Do you want to see me in your office, sir?' Pip asked the dean mildly.

'No.'

'You mean the…the incident is closed?' Pip suggested hopefully.

'Firmly closed. But not, I fancy, in the way you imply. I do not wish to see you in this hospital after the next five minutes. Nor in its vicinity. Mr Chipps, I know your father well. I admire him as a general practitioner of the best old-fashioned sort. I did my utmost here to allow you to follow in his path. I turned a blind eye to so many of your antics at St Swithin's, that I must on countless occasions have shared the affliction of our friend here in the camel-coloured dressing-gown, who would from his manner of jumping about and swearing still appear to be in considerable physical and mental suffering. This is too much, even for such a reasonable person as myself. You are expelled. You can appeal to the medical school council, but I would advise against it. I believe there is a paragraph in our original Charter from Queen Elizabeth the First, empowering the flogging of students at the front gate, if not their hanging from it.'

Pip stood staring at the floor, slowly shaking his head. 'I didn't come to St Swithin's just because my father wanted me to follow in his footsteps, you know. There's something much more important. I am simply filled with an honest desire to help sick people.'

'In which case, I suggest you apply for the job of a hospital porter,' snapped the dean. 'Please do not omit to return to my secretary the keys of your locker, or the appropriate sum of money in lieu.'

'So this is the end?' asked Pip, still unbelievingly.

'It is. Goodbye, Mr Chipps.'

Pip left the ward, sadly unbuttoning his white coat. Tony Havens and Hugo Raffles were waiting at the end of the corridor.

'How did you get on?' they both asked eagerly.

'Pipped,' said Pip.

# 5

'Matron. Sisters. Nurses. I am greatly honoured that you should ask me to officiate at this joyous occasion of presenting the student nurses' prizes.'

The dean leant slightly forward, his spread-out finger-tips touching the table, wearing an expression of infinite benevolence.

'I only wish it was an occasion which had occurred at a more joyous time for our country. *Change and decay in all around I see*, to make an appropriate quotation from Holy Writ. Well, from *Hymns Ancient and Modern*, at least,' he corrected himself. 'There is nowhere respect for Government, for Law, or for any authority whatever, sometimes even my own. Every day our peace is disturbed and our traffic jammed by a "demo" – horrible word, horrible habit. Generally by the idiotic public objecting to something which does them a lot of good, like fluoridization and vivisection. If people want to air their grievances, why can't they write letters to *The Times* like me?'

He took a sip of water. 'Violence is rife. So is vandalism, eroticism and absenteeism. Clap people in jail, and their accomplices demand "justice" – by which they mean instant release – for the "Wapping Six", or some other popular combination of geography and numerals which, to my mind, indicates exactly where a tally of villains met its deserts.'

The dean gazed for some moments at the ceiling. 'Where was I? Oh, yes. I want to tell you of a paperback book I found the other day in the hospital corridors. I mean library. It is called "1984". Quite horrifying. Though I suspect a good deal cosier than the real thing we're going to face. I see our magnificent City of London –' He waved an arm in its direction. 'A distressed area, with workers coming with their battered bowlers from the ghost towns of Sevenoaks and Guildford, the offices of our great financial institutions recycled for the manufacture by hand of plastic Beefeaters and Union Jack knickers, to sell to Japanese tourists on Tower Hill. The Bank of England preserved as a national monument like Stonehenge, the Stock Exchange turned into the National Casino its doctrinaire enemies keep calling it – '

'Lionel! You can't say all that,' objected his wife Josephine, who was laying the table round him that same Tuesday lunchtime, in the dining-room of their small house near St Swithin's.

'It's a little joke, dear.'

'You didn't say it in a very jokey voice. Your whole speech is far too gloomy for the nurses' prizegiving. You'll have to rewrite it before tomorrow night.'

'I can't help it if the whole world is on the Cresta Run to ruin,' the dean complained testily, banging the dining-table.

'You'll break a glass, dear. You should take the chance of cheering everyone up with an encouraging word, instead of passing round that the brakes have failed.'

'*Odi profanum vulgus*,' muttered the dean even more gloomily.

'What's that mean?'

'It's a polite Latin way of saying I loathe the common herd. Unfortunately, these days we have to go mooing along with the rest. Packaged tours, packaged foods, packaged views on television – ah, hello, my dear. As you were coming home for lunch today, I decided to join you,' he greeted his daughter Faith. 'I've rather eaten my way through the menu in the Bertie Bunn.'

'Did you have a lovely dance?' asked her mother, who was younger than the dean, dark-haired, soft-eyed and soft-bosomed. The dean had wooed Josephine while he was a St Swithin's registrar, in the traditional medical way. She had been a nurse on night duty, and his romantic murmurings in the shaded light, his proposal of marriage itself, were jarred only by the recumbent patients periodically breaking wind.

'The dance was fantastic.' Faith kissed her mother. 'I took hundreds of pounds for the tombola. Men seemed to be pressing money on me all evening.'

The dean frowned. 'After a life of service to humanity, I am beginning to wonder if we show misplaced generosity towards society's misfits. All these destitutes and meths drinkers and so on would be better treated by being given a good, solid day's work digging up Oxford Street.'

'Anyone there you knew?' her mother asked.

'Not a soul.'

'I would offer you both a glass of sherry,' the dean explained. 'But I am examining again this afternoon, so must keep a clear head. Not that some of the candidates wouldn't drive to drink the entire Salvation Army, with the band playing. Do you know what happened this morning?' he continued fervently. 'Sir Lancelot and I not only had to fail – that would have been a vastly inadequate penalty – but kick out of the hospital a harebrained public menace called Chipps – What's the matter?' he demanded, as Faith gave a cry.

'Nothing, Daddy. But you've spoken of him. Often.'

'Have I? Well, he was always up to some lunacy or other. Last Christmas, he brought the roast turkey into the ward in obstetrical forceps. Thank God we shan't be suffering from that particularly painful affliction any more.'

'But he might have been a simply wonderful doctor,' said Faith, whose big grey eyes had grown rounder.

'Rubbish. He doesn't know his coccyx from his epicondyle.'

'But what will he do now?' she asked, her pink cheeks becoming rosier.

'That is a matter of supreme indifference to me.'

'With all his years of studying wasted?' she insisted, her generous bosom heaving faster.

'The amount of medicine which Chipps learnt at St Swithin's hardly fits him for scrubbing the hospital floors, I assure you. In fact, today I have done the young man a service. I have stopped him becoming an utter disgrace to the profession.'

'Are you *sure* you don't know him, Faith?' asked her mother, carefully setting down the final fork.

'Oh, no, Mummy. I never mix with the students. Daddy doesn't like me to.'

'I merely want to spare you from the molestations of a bunch of drunken sex-maniacs who drive their cars too fast,' the dean explained in a reasonable tone. 'By the way, you're off from the destitutes tomorrow evening?' Faith nodded. 'I'd like you to come on the platform with your mother when I present the nurses' prizes. It will be a good opportunity to present yourself in public, being an extremely genteel one.'

'Daddy, I may have another engagement.'

'No excuses. This is a duty. You understand?'

'Yes, Daddy. I would always do whatever I see to be my duty. You taught me that,' she told him meekly.

'What are you doing in that cupboard, Josephine?' he demanded.

'Finding the sherry.'

'I told you, I'm examining this afternoon.'

'But I'm not. And please don't stare at me like Mr Pecksniff.'

The dean's prickly eyebrows rose slowly towards the point of his head, like a pair of caterpillars crawling up a turnip. 'Are you implying that I am a hypocrite?'

'Oh, no,' his wife replied lightly, producing the bottle. 'Only in danger of becoming one. You get toffee-nosed about students who might disgrace your noble profession, then you make as much money out of it as you can pocket from your private wing filled with opulent Arabs.'

The dean glared. 'Now you should like Pince, that horrible little union man.'

'There's every reason I might. He was expressing the views of a large number of people who work in St Swithin's.'

'My God,' muttered the dean. 'My wife a Communist. I'm in bed with a red. When that bottle of sherry's finished, there'll be no more, not these hard times,' he warned her as she poured a glass for herself and her daughter. 'I only bought a case of it to outwit the Chancellor of the Exchequer before the last budget. There is only one certainty one can grasp in this life, and that's the price of drink always goes up.'

'Nonsense, Lionel. You've bottles and bottles still hidden upstairs from outwitting successive Chancellors of all political hues. The whole attic looks like a skittle-alley. I think this is *cuvée* Healey,' she decided, sipping delicately. 'Though I don't think yet we've exhausted the *cuvée* Barber, or even the *cuvée* Jenkins. Which was particularly good, as I remember. Now calm down, Lionel, and let's all have a peaceful lunch.'

'I'm not very hungry, Mummy,' announced Faith. 'I had a disturbed night.'

'You shouldn't go to bed with something heavy lying on your stomach,' the dean snapped at her.

'I don't often get the chance, Daddy,' she told him demurely.

At that moment, Pip Chipps himself was drooping disconsolately at one end of the St Swithin's residents' bar. This was on the ground floor of the housemen's quarters, which with the nurses' home and the rebuilt medical school formed a screen of separate buildings set round grassy squares to the rear of the thirty-storey hospital itself. The bar was an oblong room the size of a prosperous pub, with a fruit machine, bar billiards and darts, its decorations largely portable items of corporation equipment which had appealed to the hospital rugby team as keepsakes. Along one wall were pinned a number of girls from the gonadal magazines, added arrows and technical comments indicating the customers' easy command of anatomy and gynaecology. In one corner stood a snarling, stuffed grizzly bear, Percy, the St Swithin's mascot, in whose defence against other medical schools after football matches blood had been lost, noses fractured and even richly promising girlfriends abandoned.

There were scrawled notices on a board offering for sale items as varied as motor-bikes and microscopes, guitars and gastroscopes, amplifiers and articulated hands and feet. Even the graffiti were specialized, like *You Are Never Alone With Schizophrenia, An Obstetrician is a Man who Sews Tears in Other Men's Fields*, and *Why Did the Hormone? Because She Had to Spend Her Oestrin Bed.*

Whenever the bar was open – it seemed to have developed an immunity to the licensing laws – it acted as a powerful polarizer in the St Swithin's social life. It was available to the doctors and clinical students, most of its denizens men and women under thirty. Hospitals may be depressing places to contemplate, but they are staffed essentially by the ebullient young. The residents' bar was not below a visit from the senior consultants like Sir Lancelot Spratt, or even austere professors. Dr Bonaccord, the remote, other-worldly St Swithin's psychiatrist, wandered in to relieve his inner tensions. The dean regularly tried to close it down.

'Console yourself that it was just terribly bad luck,' Hugo Raffles was sympathizing with Pip over their pints. 'After all, it was an evens chance that you picked the wrong eye.'

Pip complained in reply, 'It wouldn't have happened, if you'd never told me about that patient in the first place.'

'What ingratitude,' objected Tony Havens. 'After we'd gone to all the trouble of nosing out the cases, not to mention poncing you up when you reeled into the hospital looking like a long-lost swab.'

'You're always getting me into some sort of a mess,' Pip declared self-pityingly. 'Apart from Sir Lancelot's operating boots, there was the time you told me the dean wanted his rear bumper chained to the hospital railings because of car thieves –'

'What's a little harmless fun, dear boy?' Hugo slapped him on the shoulder. 'Surely you can take a joke?'

'No, I can't. Not really. I'm very sensitive. I think I inherit it from my mother.'

'Oh, come on,' Tony disagreed. 'We used to pull your leg because we thought you never minded. That's what made you so popular in the medical school.'

'We all love you,' Hugo assured him.

'Do you? Then find me a job.'

The two stared thoughtfully at their beer. 'That could be a problem,' confessed Tony. 'What do most ex-medical students do?'

'Go round GPs doing high-pressure salesmanship for expensive and generally useless products from the big drug companies,' Hugo told him. 'Just like the struck-off doctors do.'

Pip shook his head. 'That doesn't appeal. I'm too honest.'

'The Church?' suggested Tony. 'You wanted to be a psychiatrist. Religion these days is only practical psychiatry with singing on Sundays.'

'The Law?' added Hugo. 'You've the makings of a great coroner.'

'Don't you have to be a doctor as well?' Pip objected. 'My father says that coroners are exceptional drop-outs, who have managed to fail in two professions, not one.'

His two friends sipped their beer in nonplussed silence.

'It seems such a scandal that all the medicine I *have* managed to pick up here should be wasted,' Pip pointed out miserably. 'Just because I got an unfair reputation in the hospital for hamfistedness. I admit, I always somehow seemed to drop on the floor instruments and X-rays and the notes –'

'And sometimes the patient,' Tony reminded him.

'But I do honestly want to help people who can't help themselves. I know that's not a thing any of us care to confess at St Swithin's – particularly in the bar – but I can't see any other reason why we're here at all.'

'Anyone come up with other suggestions?' asked Hugo.

'Yes. The dean. He advised me to become a hospital porter.'

'But that's a magnificent idea,' said Tony, grinning.

'Do you think so? But what sort of hospital should I apply to?'

'Here. St Swithin's,' Tony told him. 'Just imagine the scene – you pushing a stiff down the corridor and running into the dean. It would make Stanley and Dr Livingstone look a very casual encounter.'

The two housemen started laughing so heartily that everyone near by asked to be let into the joke.

'I can just see the dean's face,' Hugo managed to say. 'As you catch him in the epigastrium with a trolley of the patients' dinners.'

'He might throw me out all over again,' said Pip, not joining in the fun.

'Impossible, dear boy,' Hugo told him. 'Porters come under the hospital administrator. The dean can't sack porters any more than Mr Clapper up in the office can reach for a scalpel and dig into the patients.'

'It *could* be rather humorous,' Pip agreed doubtfully. 'But Mr Clapper might not take me on.'

'Don't be stupid.' Tony Havens swallowed the remains of his pint. 'You speak English, and you're pink.'

# 6

'Ah, Mr Grout.' Mr Clapper, senior administrative officer of St Swithin's Hospital, stared across his broad desk at the junior administrative officer of St Swithin's Hospital early that same afternoon. 'Please sit down. I should like to go into conference with you for a few minutes.'

Mr Clapper was chubby cheeked and blue jowled, dark suited and white shirted, his black hair and shoes shining equally at both poles of his globular body. He had dark rims to his glasses, pink ones to his eyes. A faint smile always stretched his rubbery moist lips. He looked like a cat which had just eaten the cream and knew where there was plenty more.

The administration office occupied the entire first and second floors of the main St Swithin's block, and Mr Clapper was busily advancing it into the wards on the third, which he had been obliged to close to patients through shortage of domestic staff. His own room was large and airy, well-windowed on a corner of the building. Mr Grout's was a small one just outside. Mr Clapper could have summoned Mr Grout by shouting, 'Charlie!' through the door. But he had preferred to press one of the long double row of different coloured buttons on his desk, by which he could instantly demand people all over the hospital through a complicated adaptation of the normal bleeping system.

'You speak German, I believe, Mr Grout?'

'No, just a little French, Mr Clapper. *Il fait beau temps, où est les messieurs,* that sort of thing.'

The administrator frowned briefly. 'I expect both languages have many words in common. I am not a linguist. It is really an extraordinarily disorderly system, people talking quite incomprehensibly to the ears of others across the remarkably small and easily traversed area of modern Europe. I really don't see why they can't all switch to English.' He broke off, frowning more severely. 'Mr Grout –'

'Mr Clapper?'

'That shirt, Mr Grout.'

His junior peeked downwards. He was young and skinny, with sandy hair and a droopy moustache. He too was dark-suited, standing against Mr Clapper's desk with hands respectfully clasped behind him.

'I do not think, Mr Grout, that a shirt with such bold pink stripes is appropriate for our position.'

'I succumbed to temptation in the boutique,' Mr Grout apologized humbly.

'I know you are unmarried, and possibly dress to attract the other sex,' Mr Clapper said indulgently. 'But we must draw the line, surely?'

'I'll change it next washday, Mr Clapper.'

'Good. Always remember that you and I are the two most important personages in St Swithin's. Without us, the hospital would grind to a halt. Worse, it would utterly disintegrate, like a driverless express hitting the buffers. Neither forget that we are Civil Servants. The St Swithin's doctors are all Civil Servants, too,' he added, with a contemptuous little puff of his lips. 'But they refuse to recognize the fact.'

'As you often say, Mr Clapper, only eccentrics become doctors.'

Mr Clapper nodded solemnly. 'A doctor, not of medicine but of philosophy, is arriving from Hamburg on Thursday to study the working of the National Health Service. I should like you to look after him. I am of course far too busy. You may find it a somewhat uphill task, I warn you,' he continued frankly. 'I met a German doctor of philosophy once. Very eminent in his university. I thought he was a bit cracked. Well, show him round St Swithin's. You may entertain him to lunch in the canteen,' the administrator added generously. 'As long, of course, as you do not exceed the scheduled limit, and submit the appropriate docket.'

'I'll do my best to impress him, Mr Clapper,' said Mr Grout with dutiful eagerness.

'I'm sure little effort will be necessary.' A dreamy look intruded behind Mr Clapper's glasses. 'The administration of our National Health Service is a very beautiful thing, Mr Grout. You are fortunate in being too young to remember the bad old days, when St Swithin's was run in an appallingly slipshod way. There was something called a Board of Governors – rank amateurs! Well-meaning City bankers, ladies in big hats, the hospital secretary some thickwitted old Admiral or General. They convened in the Founders' Hall once a month, and had tea with buttered toast. You won't believe this, Mr Grout, but if the hospital wanted anything – a new houseman, a new scalpel, a new bedsheet – the governors had to proceed *with no help from outside whatever.*'

He leant back in his well-padded leather chair for effect. 'But today, Mr Grout, our National Health Service enjoys the most sophisticated system of administration. We know exactly where we are. The chain of command runs from the Elephant – we used to call it the Elephant and Castle, but we seem to have dropped the Castle – which contains the Department of Health and Social Security. On to the Regional Health Authorities – '

Mr Clapper extended an arm dramatically. Mr Grout knew this to be his favourite recitation. 'Then to Area Health Authorities, which may be Ordinary or Teaching. To District Management Teams! To Sector Management Teams! Finally, the power which pours from the Minister seeps into each individual hospital. All splendidly staffed by thousands upon thousands of highly trained – and, I must admit, fittingly remunerated – professional administrators. Were the whole country wiped out by plague tomorrow, the National Health Service would still be justified by the perfection of its administrative machinery.'

'New housemen or new bedlinen today,' Mr Grout reflected, 'need fourteen separate approvals.'

'Exactly,' Mr Clapper told him proudly. 'Unlimited outside help.'

'And take about four months to get.'

'Naturally, it needs time to communicate from the bottom of this ingenious structure to the top and back again. But it ensures that no action is taken with reckless haste. That will be all,' he said, with the air of a cat dismissing its mouse. 'Don't forget the shirt.'

'There's one of the students to see you, Mr Clapper.'

'He's not my pigeon, Mr Grout. Send him to the dean.'

'He's not *exactly* a student, Mr Clapper. He's failed his finals, apparently. He wants a job as hospital porter.'

Mr Clapper leant back, pudgy fingertips together. Mr Grout saw at once that he had presented his superior with an administrative problem, and one as diverting as a clue from some untaxing crossword puzzle. 'He has been expelled from the medical school? Right. Therefore he is simply a member of the general public. Agreed? Therefore he is eligible to be employed by the National Health Service, in the appropriate grade at the appropriate salary and with the appropriate deductions for his eventual old age pension. I see no difficulty. None whatsoever. We shall have the advantage of his knowing his way round the hospital.' Mr Clapper hesitated. 'Is he, er, ah – ?'

'He comes from Somerset, Mr Clapper.'

'Good!'

In the Bertram Bunn Wing few of the patients could speak English, in St Swithin's itself few of the domestic staff. The hospital enjoyed a regular supply of home-grown young graduates from its medical school, so avoiding the necessity in less favoured institutions of issuing their doctors with phrase books explaining in Oriental languages what British patients meant by such alarming complaints as, 'I've got a frog in my throat'. The St Swithin's overseas recruits were largely research workers, who could be kept harmlessly in laboratories until it was time to go home again. And everyone agreed that Sir Lancelot Spratt was unfair in claiming that, to be sure his basic surgical instructions were followed over the years, he had been obliged to learn a smattering of Hindi, Tamil, Chinese – embracing Mandarin, Cantonese, Hakka, Swatow, Foochow, Wenchos, Ning-po and Wu – Arabic, Spanish, the Pitsu of the Afghanistans, which was distinct from their Persian and unwritten Turki, Serbo-Croat, Hebrew and Gaelic. It was Mr Clapper who wished he had command of all these languages, or at least that their speakers would learn English.

'You deal with him,' directed Mr Clapper. 'I'm busy. How about references?'

'He gave the names of two West Country bishops.'

'That sounds quite reliable. Don't forget to see that he signs for his brown coat.'

Mr Grout left Mr Clapper staring pleasantly at his rows of buttons, wondering who to summon next.

'The duties appertaining to the hospital porters,' said Mr Grout, sitting behind his cheap desk and screwing up his eyes while Pip in turn stood respectfully opposite, 'are one, the movement of patients, two the movement of meals, three the movement of drugs and laundry Oh, and bodies. And of course cleaning. We have a porters' pool.'

He opened his eyes to stare at Pip. 'It's in the basement. A highly efficient system evolved by Mr Clapper, after extensive time-and-motion studies. There must always be a porter or two standing by for emergencies, but Mr Clapper has so arranged the work-schedules that none of you remain idle for more than a minimum period of time. Mr Clapper is very proud of it. Did you know that each patient in St Swithin's enjoys one-twentieth of a porter? It's well below the national peak. Mr Clapper is very proud of that, too. Report to the head porter,' he continued in a businesslike voice. 'Who will organize your training in accordance with DHSS Circular HM bracket sixty-eight bracket ninety-six. Which is of course based on the Report of the Advisory Committee on Ancillary Staff Training.'

'Training? For pushing the laundry?'

'If the Ministry say training you need, training you get,' Mr Grout told him firmly. 'National Insurance number? Tax coding?' Pip confessed himself as ignorant of both as of the Zodiacal configuration under which he was born. 'You'll have to join ACHE, of course. They operate a closed shop. See Mr Sapworth. He's due to be down in the pool in exactly two minutes.'

'I haven't a watch. It's wonderfully liberating. I wish I'd given them up years ago.'

'Never forget that the patients see more of the porters than of the doctors. As Mr Clapper says, your attitude and efficiency are of great importance to the reputation of St Swithin's. Sign here, please, for this brown coat.'

Pip left the office feeling that entering St Swithin's as a porter was more inspiring than entering it as a student. He decided that with his new status he had better take the service lift. Buttoning up his brown coat, he joined the wide, lumbering conveyance descending with bundles of dirty laundry, a refuse bin trailing blood-spattered bandages, a trolley loaded with drugs, another loaded with congealed dirty dishes, eight brown-coated porters, and two patients, one of whom was dead.

Pip wedged himself next to the porter in charge of the covered mortuary trolley, a man younger than himself with untidy dark hair, a large stylish moustache and square glasses. 'You're one of the students, ain't you?' the man asked at once, looking puzzled.

'I was. I got the chop this morning. I've just been taken on as one of you.'

'Go on?' He shook Pip's hand vigorously. 'You're the poor sod what kept getting the stick from Sir Lancelot. I reckon you're better off for the change. More free and easy, this life. I'm Harold Sapworth. Pleased to meet you.'

'I was told to report to the head porter.'

'You'll have to take a bus. There ain't one. Left last Christmas. Got a better job in a hotel. Patients don't leave tips, see.' He nodded down at his charge. 'Especially dead ones.'

'But Mr Grout in the office said – '

'Listen, mate.' Harold Sapworth grinned. 'First thing you learn about St Swithin's, them geezers in the office wouldn't know they'd been born, if they hadn't got a belly-button to prove it. Which is what they spends most of their time looking at, if you asks me. Give us a hand with this,' he invited, pushing out the trolley as the lift reached the basement.

Pip had never wasted thought on what the hospital porters got up to. They were to him simply anonymous men with complexions either black, hairy or leathery, forever pushing recumbent patients or large unidentifiable bundles on trolleys. It had never occurred to him that they were organized, the troops of a brilliantly generalled army deployed with well-drilled precision. Or were they?

'I was told to see you too, Mr Sapworth,' Pip said, pulling the front of the trolley along the wide, white-tiled, brightly lit basement corridor. 'With a view to applying for membership of ACHE.'

'No trouble. You're in.' They edged their way against a line of trolleys bringing the patients' teas from the kitchens. 'I'm filling the hole for our shop steward. He had a little accident in Piccadilly Circus.'

'I hope it won't keep him off work long,' said Pip solicitously.

'Yes, three years.'

'It must have been a nasty one.'

'It was. He was flashing. The accident was letting the coppers see him.'

'But how dreadful,' Pip commiserated over his shoulder as they continued towards the mortuary.

'Go on? What's a bit of bird?' Harold asked in surprise. 'My old dad and my brother spend most of the year inside. That's why I'm always sweating me guts out on overtime, just to keep me poor old mum.'

'Aren't you ashamed?' Pip asked involuntarily.

'Ashamed? Why? In winter, the nick's not too cold. In summer, it's not too hot. That's all there is to it.' He added in a more abrasive tone, 'You've got to get rid of all them finicky middle-class attitudes, if you're going to do a job along with us, mate.'

'I assure you I haven't any attitudes at all,' Pip replied hastily. 'I've taken great care to train myself for an open view of life. I've read a lot of Freud and Jung. I accept everybody just as they come. Most medical people do. Even Sir Lancelot.'

'That's correct,' Harold agreed thoughtfully. 'I suppose everyone looks exactly the same, seen by the tripes.'

'It's just that I haven't met many people in my sheltered life who've got fathers in jail.'

'Go on? Well, I sensed you was a good bloke,' Harold complimented him. 'The way you took all that chivvying from Sir Lancelot and that lot. If it had been me, I should have toed him in the goolies.'

They arrived at the post-mortem room, pushing through the double doors into the cool, quiet, tiled interior, its contents lying in neat sheeted rows. 'I mind your face,' said the only living occupant to Pip.

'I used to be one of the students.'

Pip recognized in the same brown coat young Forfar McBridie, a mortuary porter just joined from Glasgow. He was freckled, his brow faintly furrowed like every Scotsman's newly away from home, through the suspicion that someone was trying to swindle him or, worse still, pull his leg.

'Whose mistake's this?' he asked, indicating the trolley.

'One of Sir Lancelot's,' Harold told him.

'He won't have left much inside for us to see,' the Scotsman grumbled.

As they returned empty handed to the corridor, Pip said to Harold, 'I suppose I ought to find the porters' pool, and wait for orders?'

'Here you are, my old china.' He threw open the door of a large, low-ceilinged room fogged with tobacco and smelling of feet, its concrete floor covered with benches. It was a scene which recalled to Pip the spectators' stand of some country cricket ground on a drowsy afternoon. Men with unbuttoned brown coats and unbuttoned shirts lay or sprawled everywhere, lazily smoking, reading newspapers or paperback books, playing cards, drinking tea or cans of beer, sleeping or chatting, listening to the three or four separate programmes emerging from their radios. Peering through the haze, Pip calculated there must have been near a hundred of his new colleagues idling away their working day. He frowned. 'Are they waiting to be summoned urgently to points all round the hospital?'

'Don't be daft. You can spend days here – weeks, if you're sharp enough – without having to shift off your bum. Except for drawing your pay and tea breaks.'

'But Mr Grout in the office said there was a tremendously well-researched system –'

'Now be reasonable,' Harold told him in a pitying voice. 'It looked lovely on paper, right? A lot of schemes look lovely on paper. How to win the pools, how to win a war.' He tapped his forehead. 'They forget the human element. Get me?'

Everyone in the room suddenly rose, throwing down their reading matter and hands of cards, striding purposefully for the door. 'What's the matter?' asked Pip breathlessly. 'Some major emergency?'

'Tea break.'

'But a lot of them were already drinking tea,' Pip pointed out.

'It doesn't matter,' Harold explained in the same tone. 'It's three o'clock. Tea break. We're entitled to it. It's in our contract. Our union fought for it.'

'But supposing you just don't feel like a cup of tea? I mean, it's a little early. I generally have mine at four.'

'That makes no difference. You've still got to take your tea break. If you don't, it's a sign of workers' weakness. What happens when the workers show weakness about anything?' he added warningly. 'Even the shop temperature, one degree too high or too low. Provision of soap and towels and all that lot. Though most of these sods here would only nick them,' he remarked contemptuously as they followed the others towards the ancillary staff canteen on the far side of the building. 'A worker's weakness is a bosses' opening. Get me? It's like the old boxing match.' Harold gave a little twirl of his fists. 'Drop your guard, and you're floored. KO'd, finished. We're exploited bad enough, mate, as it is.'

'Do you know, Harold – may I call you Harold?' Pip said in an admiring voice. 'I've learned more about practical industrial relations from you in five minutes than I should have learned otherwise in a lifetime. And more than a lot of people in British business ever will learn, I suspect.'

'Go on?' said Harold, looking surprised at himself.

'It's practical mass psychiatry, that's all.'

'Listen – ' Harold briefly sucked the tip of his thumb. 'I got a bright idea. You're an educated bloke. And sharp with it. How about getting elected as our shop steward?'

'But I've hardly joined the union,' Pip protested. 'Who'd vote for me? Nobody even knows who I am.'

'Details, details,' Harold dismissed them. 'I was left in charge when Arthur Pince had his little engagement elsewhere. So I can call a branch meeting whenever I likes. Nobody attends, see? Nobody ever does. Who wants to be dragged out a night from his hearth and home and telly? Anyway, everyone always does what I says. Them Herberts,' he nodded towards their brown-coated colleagues, 'is so thick between the ears they'd thank you for doing their thinking for them. Even if it was deciding whether to go out on the booze at night or have a bit of tail off of the wife. You're on?' Pip nodded quickly. Harold shook hands again. 'No need to fix nothing more. Instant democracy, that's my speciality.'

# 7

Even without a watch, at eight o'clock promptly the following morning, the Wednesday, Pip Chipps arrived at the ancillary staff entrance at the rear of St Swithin's and punched the clock outside the gatekeeper's lodge. It was another cloudless day, threatening to be hotter than the last. Pip did not relish idling its hours away down in the smoky porters' pool. He wondered as he descended to the basement if he could somehow discover some work to perform. But there was no one to give him orders, nor even to indicate where he should seek them. He settled down with his feet up on a bench, reading Jung's *The Undiscovered Self*. Pip found interesting Jung's notion of the Socialist State taking the place of the old religions, and slavery to it a form of worship. Jung's alternative conception of socialism as a mass regression to irresponsible childhood under all-powerful parents, he marked in the margin. He wondered what such a practical socialist as Harold Sapworth would have to comment.

Pip continued his studies while his fellow-porters leisurely leafed through their copies of the *Sun*, *Mirror* or *Morning Star*, until the electric clock on the wall, which had apparently the single function of indicating the tea breaks, pointed to a few minutes after ten. He slipped the book into the pocket of his brown coat and quit the room. The administrators should have just arrived at their first-floor office.

'Yes?' Mr Grout looked up crossly as Pip's figure appeared in his doorway. 'What's the idea, barging in like that?'

Pip was taken aback. 'You didn't seem to mind when I walked in yesterday.'

'Yesterday was different. Then you were one of the students. Now you're one of the porters. I can't have hospital porters tramping in and out of my office just as they feel inclined, can I? We're worked off our feet as it is.'

'I'm sorry, Mr Grout,' he apologized meekly. 'It wasn't you I meant to disturb. I really came to see Mr Clapper.'

'Are you mad?' Mr Grout stared in outrage. 'Off your head? You, a hospital porter, demanding an audience with Mr Clapper? I've never heard of such an undisciplined, indeed insolent suggestion. Mr Clapper has far more important matters on his mind. Even porters must have enough savvy to realize that.'

Pip's normally unaggressive, easygoing, self-effacing nature turned him back to the door. Then he paused. It was not as a humble porter that he sought to enter the presence of Mr Clapper. He was himself a shining new cog in the hospital's complicated administrative machine. 'Mr Grout,' he announced modestly, 'I've just been appointed shop steward of ACHE for the whole of St Swithin's.'

'Oh, that's quite different,' Mr Grout told him briskly. 'Why didn't you say so in the first place? That was quick work, wasn't it? I suppose they wanted someone who could understand a document more complicated than a pools coupon, and was likely to keep out of jail for a bit. As shop steward, you have the right of access to Mr Clapper whenever you wish.' He picked up a red telephone on his desk and said in a humble voice, 'Mr Clapper, the shop steward would like a word with you, if it's convenient.'

'Of course it isn't convenient,' Pip heard Mr Clapper's voice clearly through the closed door between the offices. 'Can't you get rid of the fellow? Oh, well, perhaps I'd better give him some flannel. Send him in.'

Pip was greeted by Mr Clapper's pussycat smile. 'About the dartboard, is it? The one you're after in the porters' room down in the basement. A union official like yourself, Mr – ?'

'Chipps.'

'Will appreciate that these requests can't simply be pushed through any old how. They'd short circuit the administrative machinery. And dartboards are extraordinarily difficult. They don't fit into any category of hospital equipment. They are not surgical instruments. They are not furnishings. Though inspecting the necessaries for a game of darts, you might think they resembled both.'

Hands clasped across jacket button, glasses tilted ceilingwards, Mr Clapper continued speculatively, 'Dartboards are not fit and proper objects of official funds. Dear me, no. The British Treasury would never sanction the purchase of a dartboard. I am confident of that. Fortunately, the administrative machine is most adaptable – to those of us who know the right levers. I am hopeful of results under the heading of staff welfare. Or possibly nursery facilities. Or even religious ministration, which with a little ingenuity can be invoked to justify any peculiar expenditure. Rest assured, Chipps, I am pursuing the matter energetically. I write letters on the subject regularly, at least once a month.'

'It wasn't about the dartboard,' Pip said shyly. He drew a sheaf of closely written papers from his brown coat pocket. 'I stayed up all last night, working out a scheme for a more efficient use of the portering service in St Swithin's –'

'*You* worked out a scheme?' Mr Clapper rocked back in his well-padded chair, looking like a pussycat who had suffered the indignity of getting its nose caught in a mousetrap.

'Yes,' Pip nodded, spreading out his papers on Mr Clapper's impeccable blotter. 'I've found how to achieve the same amount of work in the hospital with half the number of porters. Each patient could easily get along with only one-fortieth of a porter of his own instead of a twentieth.'

'My dear young man.' Mr Clapper found himself presented with a selection of emotions, and settled for pained indulgence. 'You don't even begin to understand the research, the effort, the administrative experience, the time, the intelligence which goes into such work studies. It is obviously far beyond someone of your limited capacities and restricted education, if I may say so.'

'But it's all so easy,' Pip protested. 'You start off by sacking all the porters in the pool. Say, a hundred. You create instead a small flying squad of experienced porters, with no duties but to rush anywhere they're suddenly needed in the hospital. I sat all night going over the head porter's records, until he left last year –'

'Left? Nobody told me. He can't possibly have left.'

'And found that emergency calls for porters averaged ten point seven-five per day, less than one every two hours, you understand. Each job needed an average of five men and lasted an average of twenty minutes, so that five porters in the vast pool downstairs are, by simple arithmetic, kept in idleness for all but three of each twenty-four hours, while the remainder are kept in an idleness which is absolute.'

Pip waited patiently for comment. But it seemed Mr Clapper was in no mood for statistics. 'Will you kindly leave?' he asked coldly.

'You're not interested?' Pip asked in surprise.

'Your function in the hospital is to represent the members of ACHE, not to teach me my job.'

'I was only trying to help – '

'This is a *hospital*, Chipps. You may not understand, but it is a place where ignorant meddling can be dangerous or even fatal.'

'But won't you even read it?' Pip asked plaintively.

'You can if you like leave your outpourings with Mr Grout.' Mr Clapper made a gesture as though flicking water from his fingertips. 'I would also remind you that even shop stewards are not above dismissal for meddling in activities beyond their abilities. Good morning.'

Pip was at first mystified more than offended. He left the administration office and took the service lift, which contained half a dozen other porters, the remains of several wards' breakfasts, a superior-looking girl with the library trolley, a man smoking a pipe selling newspapers, and a nurse with a woman at the extremity of pregnancy groaning in a wheelchair. He felt sudden resentment at such highhanded rejection of a scheme, worked out so painstakingly in Faith's cubicle until they both dropped exhausted to sleep, which could save St Swithin's and the National Health Service so many thousands of pounds. There was a more liberal mentality in the wards, he reflected. The humblest student daring to question a diagnosis or line of treatment was encouraged rather than squashed. Even Sir Lancelot Spratt, Pip recalled, would grunt and declare generously, 'Well, a pup often smells a rabbit quicker than an old dog.' And at that moment, to Pip's alarm Sir Lancelot himself stepped impatiently into the waiting lift.

Sir Lancelot did not notice his former examinee. His attention was distracted immediately by a small, grey-haired, seedy-looking, thin, coloured man in red-striped flannel pyjamas and a St Swithin's-issue blue towelling dressing-gown, who pushed into the lift while the doors were starting to close.

'Sir Lancelot Spratt –' said the new arrival breathlessly, as they began to descend.

'Correct.' Sir Lancelot looked down at him, stroking his beard. 'I know you, don't I? One of the patients from Shoreditch?'

'No, no, much farther,' said the man in agitation. 'From Shanka.'

'That's it. The case Professor Ding is waiting to perform a cardiac transplant upon.'

'That is all wrong,' he declared in an urgent low voice. 'I am not his patient. I am his brother-in-law.'

Sir Lancelot was puzzled. 'The two conditions are not incompatible, I should imagine?'

'But I am not ill. There is nothing wrong with me. Nothing whatever.' The little man banged his chest hard, producing a drumlike noise. 'You hear? I am as sound as a flea.'

'But come! Professor Ding distinctly told me just two mornings ago that you were suffering from a complicated form of congenital heart defect. One which I thoroughly agree sees its only hope of relief in cardiac transplantation.'

'I will not have an operation, not on my life,' the patient said frantically.

'You are not showing much gratitude to Professor Ding,' Sir Lancelot said severely to the man wedged tight against his stomach. 'For bringing you all this way, doubtless at great expense, so that your operation might be performed in our own well-equipped hospital.'

'My heart is in the right place,' he protested bitterly. 'Listen, please, Sir Lancelot Spratt. You must help me. That assassin who runs our country wants to win the Nobel Prize. So he says to Professor Ding, "Boy, you gotta get plenty medical renown. Do some heart transplants and get in the newspapers, like all the other cutters." Professor Ding! Do a heart transplant! I wouldn't trust him to cut my toenails, between you and me, Sir Lancelot. But Professor Ding must have a try. Or he'll end up deader than…deader than I'm going to be in the next fortnight,' he ended, wiping his eyes with the back of his hand.

The lift stopped at the ground floor, and the occupants started unloading themselves. Pip stayed inside, wedged behind the breakfast-trolleys. Sir Lancelot and the man in the towelling dressing-gown stepped into the main hall.

'But good grief –' Hands deep in jacket pockets, Sir Lancelot started strolling towards the front door. 'Why did you fall in with this plan? Which strikes me as more like premeditated murder than most surgery.'

'I didn't fall in with it. I had to. The President would have had me shot otherwise. I thought it wisest to travel to London, then escape. He never liked me, Professor Ding,' the patient added. 'I don't think any man likes his brother-in-law.'

'My, my. There you are. I just wondering where you got to.' The beaming Professor Ding appeared from the direction of the entrance doors, taking his patient in a fiercely affectionate grasp by the arm. 'You just going for a little stroll after breakfast, I guess? Now, now, you naughty man,' he chortled, waving a finger vigorously under the other's nose. 'I tell you, don't I? You gotta stay in your nice, comfortable, sterile St Swithin's bed, till some unlucky geezer gets himself run over or similar, then the fun begins, eh?'

'You never mentioned that you two were related,' remarked Sir Lancelot.

'Related?' Professor Ding looked amazed, then grinned broadly. 'Sure we're related. We got the famous doctor–patient relationship.'

He laughed loudly for the best part of a minute.

'The doctor–patient relationship,' he managed to repeat at last. 'Them's the best relations in the whole world. They don't go stay in each other's houses. They don't go borrow money off each other. Not like as if they was someone's brother-in-law, hey?'

'But am I to understand that he *is* your brother-in-law?' Sir Lancelot asked in a more peppery voice, noticing that the Professor's spirit of fun caused him to poke his miserable-looking companion several times in the ribs with his fist.

'Maybe he is. Who knows? In Shanka we got as many wives as we can afford, like you in England with cars and golf clubs and similar.' Professor Ding laughed again, giving his patient another pummelling. 'People sick with the heart trouble get screwy ideas, Sir Lancelot. I guess you know that.' The professor tapped his own forehead. 'It's the anoxia. Come on, my good fella. We ride right up again in the lift to the ward, I'll go and sit right in there with you. We'll have a nice game of Scrabble, until some stupid bugger get himself run over, then it's Hey ho! Off to work we go.'

The little man gave Sir Lancelot an agonizedly imploring look. But the only action of the St Swithin's surgeon was to raise his bushy eyebrows and shrug his broad shoulders. Sir Lancelot knew how a man could steel himself for a major operation, then try and dodge when it became imminent, ingeniously parading some excuse which left his courage unquestioned. He had heard before of dissuading wives and friends, of amazing recoveries in health, of miraculous visits to faith healers, all propounded as the scalpel of Damocles was about to descend. The ebullient Ding was perhaps not the stereotype of a surgical professor, Sir Lancelot reflected as he pushed through the wide front door. But he supposed that in such an uninhibited and unruly country as Shanka a certain informality in professional manner was hardly noticeable.

# 8

Shortly before one o'clock that lunchtime, Pip took off his brown coat, threw it over his shoulder, and stepped into the residents' bar. As he expected, his two old friends were leaning with pint mugs in their usual corner.

'Come to collect the empties?' called Tony Havens at once, grinning.

'Seen the dean yet?' asked Hugo Raffles eagerly.

'I've hardly seen anyone at all. You'd be amazed at life below stairs in this hospital. Do you know exactly what I do? Sit on my backside all day with about a hundred other porters, down in the basement. Doing absolutely nothing all day long, except taking tea breaks.'

'The theatre porters will be demanding tea breaks during operations next,' Tony suggested. 'I can just hear Sir Lancelot saying, "Scalpel," then the hooter blowing and everyone walking out, leaving the patient all alone connected to the automatic respirator.'

'But it's really quite a scandalous system,' Pip insisted. 'It's a terrible waste of money for the Health Service, and it's definitely bad for staff morale.'

'The Government possesses unlimited money, dear boy, and the porters possess unlimited sloth,' Hugo told him. 'So what's the odds? There are much more worthy things to reform in the hospital. We residents could do with a squash court, for a start.'

'But portering is an essential hospital service,' Pip countered earnestly. 'In the 1963 Report of the King Edward's Hospital Fund, which I read last night, it stated that the planning and supervision of portering was of fundamental importance, and much overlooked.'

'When you're working a hundred hour week as a houseman,' Tony told him briskly, 'you've more on your mind than the mental health of the hospital porters.'

'Porters are people,' Pip murmured. He was disappointed. He had innocently expected them to be spellbound by his experiences.

'We really must fix this confrontation with the dean,' Hugo continued. 'With of course as many of the lads present as possible. Perhaps you could fix wheeling in the patient for his clinical demonstration? That's in the lecture theatre this afternoon. It would provide a delightfully dramatic setting. Then you can push off and find this lucrative job with a drug company or tin leg maker or whatever.'

'I'm not so sure that I don't just want to stay a hospital porter.'

'Oh, come, a joke's a joke,' Tony said.

'It's very edifying, seeing hospital work from the underside.'

'You must be mad,' Hugo told him. 'I'd rather be an abortionist's tout. The rake-off's better.'

'Nobody pays any attention at all to the ancillary staff,' Pip complained. 'The doctors at St Swithin's seem to think they're the only people who matter in the whole place.'

'You're right. We are,' Tony agreed.

'Why, I might even rise to be head porter in time,' Pip suggested. 'You two would be consultants by then, I suppose.'

'Maybe. But not at St Swithin's,' Tony declared. 'We're both emigrating.'

Pip looked surprised. 'When did you decide this?'

'Over the past five or six months. Hugo and I seem to have talked about nothing else. Have we?'

'You never mentioned it to me,' he objected.

'We rather lost touch with you, Pip, after we qualified last Christmas and you were still a student,' he explained condescendingly.

'San Francisco or Sydney, St Tropez or even Sark,' Hugo speculated. 'Anywhere to get out of this country, where the shortage of people who actually practise medicine is matched by the abundance of administrators telling us how to do it.'

'We're going somewhere doctors are still respected. Instead of finding themselves at the beck and call of a public who's never had anyone to order about in their lives before, and rather take to the experience.'

'To lands where money is pumped into medical research, instead of broken-down shipyards and motor-bike factories to keep bone idle workers in overpaid jobs.'

'Where the patients are obese, and so are the fees.'

'A nice little surgical clinic in upstate New York would do me,' Hugo suggested. 'The Yanks go for English doctors. We apparently have such a cheery way of telling people they're going to die.'

'I don't think I'd care to desert the ship,' said Pip solemnly. 'Even though it's sinking so fast the rats have to swim upwards.'

'Come off it, Pip,' Tony scoffed. 'What's a house job in a British hospital these days? It's a perch, before flying off to fresh woods and pastures new. There's no point staying at home longer than to learn the surgical ropes. And British doctors are not the only ones on the move. We shall be replaced by the equally great migration from the medical schools of the East.'

'You know, I think it's an entirely natural phenomenon,' said Hugo thoughtfully. 'This global east to west movement of doctors across the northern hemisphere. Do you suppose it's something to do with the Trade Winds?'

'So in the end everybody's happy,' Tony decided. 'We British doctors are happy, because we finish up with enormous cars and swimming pools and stupendous life insurance. The Eastern doctors are happy, because Cricklewood is altogether less crowded and smelly than Calcutta. So please don't make cracks about rats, Pip. Though to my mind, the rats were obviously the most intelligent beings on board.'

'But what about the welfare of the patients?' Pip asked.

'Screw the patients,' said Hugo.

Tony Havens ordered two more beers.

'What about me?' complained Pip. 'I haven't had a drink at all yet.'

The other two exchanged glances.

'Pip, dear boy,' said Hugo, 'Tony and I were discussing this very matter before you came in. As you know, this bar is a club. That's some technicality to do with the liquor licence, I believe. It's restricted to the medical staff and the medical students. Not the porters. Sorry about that.'

'Don't talk such balls,' Pip objected crossly. 'You know we've had all sorts in here. Policemen, firemen, newspaper reporters, peculiar people from television —'

'Signed in as guests,' said Tony.

'Then why can't I be signed in as a guest? I'll pay for my own drinks, if that's what you're afraid of.'

There was another silence. 'Look, Pip,' Tony continued. 'We'd love to buy you unlimited drinks. But they'll have to be in the pub down the road. You see, you *are* a porter. And if we let you come and drink here, all the other porters will want to.'

'We've had this trouble before,' Hugo added. 'Some dreadful little oik down there in the basement had the ruddy nerve to ask old Clapper why he and his fellow-workers couldn't come in here and booze away to their hearts' content. I'm sure you see the fundamental pathology? No one would object to the odd porter coming in for a pint. But with the workers, it's not only a case of one-out-all-out, it's of one-in-all-in. If we let you put a foot in the door, those bloody-minded barrack-room lawyers downstairs would cash in. You must know their "I'm all right, Doc," attitude, better than I do. The residents would be paying for your breaching the dyke long after you'd gone off to find yourself a decent job.'

'What was the name of that horrible piece of work?' Tony frowned. 'Sapworth, that's it. Some arrogant little sod to do with the union.'

Pip drew himself up. 'Mr Harold Sapworth is *not* an arrogant little sod. Or even a horrible piece of work. He is suffering from a somewhat disorganized home life, which would drive anyone of less resilient personality to suicide, or possibly murder. He enjoys instead a healthy mental attitude and a sound grasp on the essentials of life. Also, he loves his mother. And further, he happens to be one of my personal friends. Not to mention one of my close colleagues in the trade union movement.'

'You haven't joined ACHE?' they both asked in horror.

'I am the shop steward,' Pip told them with dignity.

'Pip, you're suffering from illusions,' Tony said anxiously. 'How about you and me taking a little stroll to see Dr Bonaccord?'

'On the contrary, for the first time I am beginning to see life clearly. I shall seek our Mr Sapworth and take him for a beer in the nearest public bar. Where we shall plot how to speed up the inevitable collapse of the capitalist system, as prognosticated by the clear-sighted if somewhat excitable K. Marx in the British Museum Reading Room. Workers of the world, unite.' He raised his clenched fist. 'You have nothing to pull but your chains. Sending you lot down the plughole,' he directed enthusiastically at his friends.

He strode from the bar.

Pip had left Harold Sapworth lying on a bench in the porters' pool, reading a girlie magazine and munching beetroot sandwiches. He supposed that his fellow porter would be remaining there until the next tea break. He was surprised on entering the tiled basement corridor to find Harold behind a vast bouquet wrapped with cellophane and trailing coloured ribbon.

'They got me a job to do,' he explained gloomily. 'Bunch of flowers to deliver to that bird Brenda Bristols.'

'What, the actress?' Pip said spiritedly. 'Lucky man. I wouldn't mind the chance of meeting her. Particularly sitting up in bed.'

'Go on?' Harold sucked the top of his thumb. 'You can help me out, then. I said I'd nip down to the betting shop for the lads before the first race. Wouldn't like to be late. They'd get proper stroppy if one of them was on a winner.'

'Which ward's she in?' Pip asked, taking the flowers.

'She's not in St Swithin's actual. Not the likes of her. She's ritzing it in the Bertie Bunn Wing. You'll know your way around.'

'I've never been inside the Bertie Bunn in my life,' Pip told him.

No student had. Unlike the National Health patients in St Swithin's, private ones were not liable to be abruptly set upon by twenty or thirty young men and women in white coats, prodding and pummelling and discussing what was wrong between themselves as though the object of their attention had already succumbed to the death which he now gathered was swiftly inevitable.

'Go on? It's got colour telly and that, and they has their veg served separate.'

'But hasn't it got porters of its own?'

'Suppose not. They don't have doctors and nurses of their own, do they? It's all worked out somewhere under the National Health.'

'But don't you object, taking flowers to private patients?'

'Never thought about it, really. I must get on and place them bets.'

'Perhaps you'd join me for a drink this evening after work, Harold?' Pip remembered. 'In the local. I expect you'd really prefer the residents' bar?' he added pointedly.

'Wouldn't go near that place. I hear the beer's gnat's piss and the prices is shocking.'

Pip looked puzzled. 'But surely, you headed a campaign to have porters allowed in it?'

'That was only a matter of principle.'

'I see.' Pip nodded several times. 'Like not dropping your guard in boxing? Or to be more exact, aiming a crafty punch where it would hurt most?'

'That's right, mate. You're learning fast,' said Harold admiringly. 'Give a big kiss from me to Brenda Bristols.'

# 9

As Pip started out with her flowers from the basement of St Swithin's, Brenda Bristols was sitting up in bed against a bank of pillows, in a plunging transparent nightie, sipping a vodka martini and reading *Private Eye* while waiting for her lunch. The door of her room flew open, revealing a short pink man in glasses, dressed in a plain white nightshirt reaching half-way down his lumpy thighs, crying, 'Help me!'

Brenda Bristols looked at him over her magazine. A career enlivened with sex-obsessed actors, wild-eyed directors, passionate playwrights and groping millionaires in nightclubs all over the world had left her unconcerned with life's sexual vicissitudes. 'Hello,' she said amiably.

'Help me,' repeated her visitor.

'Would you like me to buzz for a nurse?' Or has your telly gone wrong?'

'Dear lady! Please help me. May I come in?'

He slammed the door behind him, trotting across the thick apricot-coloured carpet to the high white bed designed by earnest and ingenious Swedes, with buttons and handles jutting all over it for placing patients instantly in a dozen different positions, all of them uncomfortable. He looked round wildly. 'Where can I hide?'

'There's my bathroom.' She nodded towards a second door. 'It's a little clammy.'

'You don't lead to the fire escape?' he asked desperately, eyes falling on the sunlit balcony. 'Or perhaps I could make a rope of sheets?'

'I don't really think I can spare the ones I'm using.'

'I suppose it *is* seven storeys down. I should have to borrow dozens of them. And that would of course attract attention.'

'Don't you think it might also attract attention,' Brenda Bristols mentioned, 'even these informal days, running through the City of London in your little nightie?'

'Perhaps you could lend me something?' His eyes gleamed. 'I could effect my escape in what they call drag. Yes, like Bonnie Prince Charlie with Flora Macdonald.'

'I don't think anything of mine would fit you terribly well, darling. But where are your own?'

'They hid them. Last night. When they stuck me in the room across the corridor. I wanted to get out. My chauffeur was waiting. He probably still is.'

Brenda Bristols tossed aside her *Private Eye*. 'But they can't *keep* you in here, sweetie. Unless you can't pay your bill. Then I suppose they make you wash up the bedpans, or something.'

'Oh yes, they can.' He grabbed her hand with both of his. 'I'm a computer case.'

She sipped her martini in the other hand. 'I do hope it's not painful?'

'It's a terrible thing to suffer,' he told her, cheeks shaking. 'The computer downstairs diagnosed me as an acute schizophrenic with hay fever and pregnancy.'

'You don't look noticeably pregnant to me,' she decided, inspecting him. 'But I suppose you're only a few weeks gone?'

'I'm only repeating what the computer said,' he told her miserably, still clutching her hand. 'And I *knew* I had hay fever. I didn't need any beastly computer to rub it in. I've suffered horribly from it for years. Then it decided for some reason of its own that I was pregnant.' He gave a harsh laugh. 'So it decided that I must be suffering from delusions. That I was off my head. The computer never decided that it was off *its* head. Oh, no! It's too arrogant, self-opinionated, ruthless and utterly inhuman. It's got a personality exactly like both my former wives,' he ended bitterly.

'But surely,' she pointed out calmly, 'you can just tell one of the doctors that some slight computerized error has been made? Like with your gas bill?'

'You can't. That's the basic trouble,' he said frantically. 'Apparently, once you start with the computer finding what's wrong with you, the ordinary human doctor simply can't interfere. If the computer makes a mistake, it's supposed to sort itself out. The doctor would have to start from scratch, plodding away to find what you've got. When you quite likely haven't got anything at all. I shall just have to stay until the computer has the common decency to admit it's wrong. I shall probably spend the rest of my life here.'

'It's deliciously comfortable.'

'But the expense! It makes Claridge's look like Butlin's.'

'Have a drink. The ice is in the fridge under the telly.'

He poured himself half a tumbler of vodka from the bottle at her bedside and gulped it down. 'Surely we've met before?' he asked more calmly.

'I'm Brenda Bristols. You've probably seen me on the box.'

'Of course. I caught you in *This Is Your Life*. Tell me, did you know that compère fellow was disguised as a cow when you thought you were opening The Dairy Show?'

He sat on the edge of the high bed, glass in one hand, demurely tugging down the edge of his nightshirt across his hairy thighs with the other. 'I'm Lord Hopcroft. You've probably seen me in the financial pages,' he said modestly. 'I own hotels.'

'But how nice. Fix me another drink, sweetie, will you? Lunch seems late.'

'Complain to the *maître d'hôtel*,' he counselled, pouring her a martini. 'Or I suppose it would be the *maître d'hôpital*? I imagine this is all in order?' he asked doubtfully, opening the refrigerator for the ice, his original agitation subsiding. 'I mean, here am I, a member of the House of Lords, well respected in City circles, trotting about a strange woman's bedroom wearing only a nightshirt apparently designed for hospitalized dwarfs. If it got in the newspapers –'

'But we're sickly, not sexy,' she pointed out.

'You know what newspapers can make of the most innocent situation,' he said, returning with the glass.

'Be a love and let down the end of my bed while you're passing. The young little doctor-man seemed to want my feet in the air. But it'll turn into an enormous armchair for eating. You press that red knob just underneath,' she indicated.

'This?'

Lord Hopcroft touched the red button. With an obedient purr, the bed see-sawed its foot steadily into the air, tipping on the apricot carpet the bank of pillows, the vodka martini and *Private Eye*. 'How dreadfully clumsy of me,' remarked Lord Hopcroft, as these contents were followed by Brenda Bristols.

'Worse accidents happen in hospitals, I suppose,' she said philosophically. She sat on the floor beside him, as the bed halted almost vertically.

'What amazing telescopic legs,' he murmured, as they both peered underneath. 'I always thought my second wife possessed those. She managed to keep a remarkably sharp eye on my activities at cocktail parties. Shall I press this yellow button?'

There was another whirr. The bed tipped sharply sideways on top of them. 'We're trapped!' he exclaimed, struggling to escape. 'This hospital is absolutely dominated by its mechanical devices.'

'Can't you reach the other button with your toes?' Brenda Bristols asked irritably, as they lay pressed together like two flowers in a book.

'I don't think I can. I really must apologize if I'm rather warm. It's a very hot day.' There was a knock on the door. Lord Hopcroft cried with alarm, 'Nobody must see us like this.'

'It's only the girl with my lunch,' she said impatiently. 'And *some*body's got to get us out, haven't they? *Please* come in,' she called.

Pip entered in his brown coat, bearing the flowers.

A man's opinions are formed less by events than the mood in which he discovers them. Karl Marx might have concurred about capitalism with John D. Rockefeller, had his theory not been conceived in the arid leathery womb of the British Museum Reading Room. Pip had that afternoon noticed for the first time the lines of Rolls-Royces parked outside the Bertram Bunn Wing, discovered its expensive shop, eyed its extravagant interior decoration, heard the soft music and felt the soft carpeting, jostled against the hurrying trays of savoury-smelling food and expensive bottles in baskets or dewy buckets. Three days before, it would all have brought hardly a shrug to his narrow shoulders. Now he saw everywhere pampering rather than nursing, comfort overlying cure, money before medicine. In the mood which had glowed and flamed within him that morning, he found it shockingly unjust that human beings with exactly the same diseases, undergoing exactly the same treatment in exactly the same hospital, should enjoy conditions as different as Dingley Dell from Dotheboys Hall.

'Oh, sorry,' he said. Further, private patients indulged in frolics certainly not to be countenanced by a St Swithin's ward sister. 'May I leave the flowers?'

'My gentleman friend and myself are not, in fact, enjoying ourselves very much.'

'We're trapped in the jaws of this bed,' Lord Hopcroft told him.

'Could you be awfully useful and summon some assistance?'

Pip's mind had been trained as a medical student in the wards of St Swithin's to dissect and assess the elements of all alarming situations, then to take swift remedial action. He dropped the flowers and pushed a button on the wall, set in a red ring marked EMERGENCY. At once a light flashed and a bell shrilled outside the open door. He stood looking down sympathetically, waiting for someone to appear. Nobody did.

'Can't you make a rather more active sort of effort?' Brenda Bristols complained.

Pip strolled round to the other side of the bed. 'There's a handle,' he announced, starting to crank it. As the pair struggled free, a female voice came crossly from the corridor, '*Why* do patients keep pushing the emergency button by mistake? Anyone would think the nursing staff had nothing to do all day.'

'The bathroom!' exclaimed Lord Hopcroft, leaping in and shutting the door.

'What *are* you doing, Porter?' demanded the blue-uniformed matron, hurrying into the private room with cap streamers flying and flicking off the alarm. 'And what are *you* doing, Miss Bristols? I don't remember giving you permission to get out of bed. Oh, let me attend to it, you clumsy fool,' she continued impatiently, seizing the handle from Pip. 'Look what you've done to this patient. You might easily have fractured several of her vertebrae. You porters must not meddle with these beds, which need a certain amount of intelligence to operate. There, see how quickly *I*'ve got it straight –' She stared and blinked. 'Pip! What are you doing in this room? In that coat?'

'Oh, hello, Auntie Florrie,' he replied mildly. 'I work here.'

'I know you do.' She stamped a stoutly shod foot. 'Why aren't you taking your exams?'

'I failed.'

'How utterly disgraceful.'

'I'm sorry –'

'When I specifically instructed Sir Lancelot Spratt to pass you.'

'Dear Sir Lancelot,' murmured Brenda Bristols, slipping gracefully back into bed. 'The bear with the swansdown hug.'

'You may claim a personal relationship with your surgeon,' said the matron, ignoring Pip to jerk her patient forward and slam the pillows behind her back. 'But I should like you to know that it cuts absolutely no ice whatever with me. Nor that you are a national figure, having your photograph with no clothes on displayed in every lorry-driver's caff up and down the country.'

'Charming, how you go round cheering up the patients, Matron,' she said silkily.

'I regard you simply as another female in my care. Like those of any age, any appearance and any profession in the Bertram Bunn Wing.' The matron pounded the pillows savagely. 'All are exactly the same to me. I am a dedicated nurse. Aren't I, Pip?'

'Then perhaps you'd hand me my lunch?' Brenda Bristols nodded towards the green-overalled girl standing uncertainly with a tray in the doorway. 'I'm starving.'

'Auntie Florrie –' began Pip.

'Shut up,' the matron told him, plonking the tray on the actress' knees.

'Ugh,' said Brenda Bristols. 'Cold vichyssoise. Always gives me the gripes.'

'If you don't want it, you needn't have it,' said the matron furiously. 'I'll throw it down the loo.' She opened the door of the bathroom. 'What are *you* doing here?' she demanded, as Lord Hopcroft sidled shyly into the room, both hands holding the hem of his nightshirt tight across the top of his legs.

'I came to borrow some toothpaste,' he explained.

'*Miss* Bristols! Why have you a half-naked man in your room?'

'He's my guru.'

'Auntie Florrie –'

'Shut up. When were you admitted?' she demanded of Lord Hopcroft. 'What's your diagnosis?'

'I'm several months in the family way.'

'My brain is going.' The matron drew the back of her hand across her forehead. 'It's all the sheikhs and their habits. I should have stayed in the National Health wards, where the patients at least do what they're told.'

'Auntie Florrie –'

'Shut up.'

'Auntie Florrie, I refuse to shut up.' The determination was so unusual for Pip, she rocked back on her heels. 'Did I understand you to say that you canvassed Sir Lancelot to pass me in my surgery clinical?'

'Of course I did,' she replied shortly. 'You'd never have got through by your own unaided efforts in a month of very wet Sundays.'

'Thank you very much,' he told her sharply. 'Now I know your opinion of my mental abilities.'

'Don't get all dignified, Pip, please,' she said impatiently. 'I have tolerated you as an amiable half-wit for years. So has the rest of the family, with the calamitous if understandable exception of your adoring parents. Now look here, Miss Bristols,' she switched her attention. 'Your charms may be flaunted in every Underground station, where I might add the public draw on many interesting additions –'

'Auntie Florrie!' shouted Pip. 'I may be a halfwit, but I was dedicated to becoming a doctor. And through my own efforts, if you don't mind. You have bossed me and my poor parents about quite mercilessly for years.'

'Pip, you must try and control your vile temper. It only makes you utter insulting falsehoods which you immediately regret. Miss Bristols, you may be meat and drink to Lord Longford and Mrs Mary Whitehouse –'

'Auntie Florrie, you're a two-faced prig.'

She stared speechless.

'Yes, you are.' Pip was carried away. 'You're a complete phoney. You boast you're a dedicated nurse. What do you do? Run a clinical clip joint. This wing charges breathtaking prices, and I'll tell you exactly why. Because the National Health Service has become so ramshackle that a lot of people will pay almost anything, even all their savings, just to escape its clutches.'

'Please keep that sort of talk for your disreputable friends,' she said icily.

'I shall,' Pip returned firmly. 'You wait and see.' He raised his clenched fist. 'Porter Power!'

He left. He heard behind him an enthusiastic burst of applause from Brenda Bristols.

# 10

'Harold –' Pip came running in the sunshine back to the main block of St Swithin's. He saw that his fellow-porter was unlucky enough to be burdened with another job that afternoon. Harold Sapworth was slowly pushing a low trolley loaded with crates marked MEDICAL SUPPLIES – URGENT into the goods entrance at the rear of the hospital. 'Can you spare a minute?'

'Long as you like, mate.' Harold leant on the handle of his trolley and pulled an emaciated home-rolled cigarette from the top pocket of his brown coat. 'No hurry. Got all day, if you want.' He struck a match. 'Where you bin? Out for a few pints? You looks pink around the chops.'

'I am drunk, but with indignation.'

'Go on?'

'I delivered those flowers in the Bertram Bunn Wing. I had an altercation with the matron.'

'Go on?'

'The Bertram Bunn Wing is a towering social injustice, which should be demolished.'

'Go on?'

'*Please* don't keep saying "Go on" like that, Harold. Haven't you any opinions of your own?'

'You gets good tips there. Some of them wogs hand out quids like they was Green Shield stamps.'

'Harold, I implore you to raise your eyes from the mud to the stars.' Harold Sapworth dutifully looked upwards. 'Now let me get this absolutely right. The same porters, cooks and bottlewashers serve the

Bertie Bunn as the St Swithin's National Health patients? The same telephonists put through their calls from the central hospital switchboard? If the Bertie Bunn went up in flames, exactly the same hospital firemen would carry all the sheikhs out over their shoulders? But do these porters, cooks, firemen and so on realize how they're being exploited?'

'Shouldn't think so. Most of 'em can't speak English.'

'Harold, I am going to hold a branch meeting of the union,' declared Pip, clapping his companion on the shoulder.

'Hold it here and now, if you like. No trouble. You and me'll do. Pass a resolution, write it in the book. Arthur Pince and me worked it like that for years. Mind, Arthur was a gaffers' man. Still, he had problems of his own.'

'*That's* not democracy, Harold. That's not what Oliver Cromwell, Earl Grey, Benjamin Disraeli, William Ewart Gladstone and Clem Attlee fought for.'

'Go on?'

'What the great Reform Bills gave the British people in the last century, we shall give the workers of St Swithin's today. That is, a say in the decisions which dominate their lives. I see my duties as shop steward as primarily educative rather than executive. I'll book the Founders' Hall for tonight. What's a convenient time? Seven o'clock?'

'No one will come,' said Harold gloomily. 'Especially if there's something good on the telly.'

'I shall make them come,' said Pip earnestly. 'I'll go right through the hospital crying, "Workers Awake!" '

'Won't be popular down below, this weather,' Harold grumbled. 'Afternoons, most of 'em doze off.'

A few minutes later, Pip was knocking deferentially at the door of Mr Grout's office on the first floor.

'If it's about the dartboard,' said the junior administrator as Pip was admitted, 'Mr Clapper is away for the afternoon playing – playing host to a very important conference at Sunningdale.'

'I want to convene a meeting of ACHE.'

'That should present no administrative difficulty.' Mr Grout reached into his glass-fronted bookshelf. 'Let me see, General Whitley Council Handbook…Paragraph one, "No obstacles should be put in the way of granting facilities for staff organizations participating in meetings…" What notices do you intend to display?' he asked, looking up. 'They should be submitted to my prior approval, but permission to exhibit should not be unreasonably withheld.'

'I don't think there'll be time for any notices,' Pip said doubtfully. 'I wanted the Founders' Hall for seven this evening.'

'It doesn't say you *have* to stick up notices,' Mr Grout agreed, peering into the book. 'That's all right, then.'

'There's just one thing – '

'Yes?'

'Why are private patients treated in National Health hospitals?'

'Because of Section Five of the National Health Service Act, 1946, as amended in the Health Services and Public Health Act, 1968. Charges by medical or dental practitioners were delimited under Circular S I 1966 stroke one five five three good afternoon,' said Mr Grout, turning his eyes dismissively down to his blotter.

In his evangelical tour of the hospital, Pip quickly discovered that Harold Sapworth had a sure grasp on the opinions of his flock. Many of the union members understood only the languages of Continental Europe or Asia. Of his compatriots, most asked who was going to pay their bus fare back to the hospital after work, and didn't they see enough of the bleeding place anyway? Pip explained that ACHE was becoming a shining example of participation in democracy, like the cities of ancient Attica. They replied that they didn't give a monkey's, so long as it landed the next pay claim.

The busy afternoon hurried past. Pip wished he'd still a watch.

The dean of St Swithin's, too, was preoccupied. At six-forty-five he was on his feet declaring, 'Matron, Sisters. Student nurses. Happy prize winners. Even in this moment of jubilation, it behoves us to ask, what sort of future do you smiling, innocent girls face? What sort of future do we all face, if it comes to that? In the thought-provoking words of Henry Francis Lyte, "The darkness deepens, earth's joys grow dim, its glories pass away." I certainly see nothing but catastrophe, on either hand. Total and inescapable. For our country and for the entire world. The precious edifice of Law has been demolished by modern brutishness like…like Coventry Cathedral. Yes, that's rather good. Like Coventry Cathedral. The former Cathedral, of course. Not the new one, which between you and me I thought rather an ecclesiastical Odeon. That's rather good, too. It is all very amusing for some of us to "Do our own thing", as it is sometimes put, I believe. But when doing our own thing is "mugging" – as I believe it is also put – old ladies in the streets at midnight, and coming out on strike whenever we happen to feel like it, then responsible members of society like myself what are you doing in that cupboard?' he demanded across his dining-room to his wife.

'Getting a gin. You don't expect me to face the nurses' prizegiving cold sober, I hope?' She held up the bottle. 'This is *cuvée* Maudling, I think. Or even Selwyn Lloyd. That was a *very* good year. Besides, Faith wants a drink, too,' she added, as their daughter appeared in the doorway.

'I disapprove of young women imbibing spirits like Hogarth's washerwomen,' the dean declared with unexpected mildness. 'But I must admit my heartfelt pleasure at your being with us this evening, Faith. I don't believe you've enjoyed the experience of hearing me speak in public before? Fleet Street will be there,' he added proudly. 'I am fortunately treating a young gentleman of the Press for a nervous gut, and he has agreed to attend. I believe he only writes the tittle-tattle column, but through the miracles of mass communications even *his* words are winged throughout the country between its cocoa and its cornflakes. I can assure you that this prizegiving will stay in your memory. Are you dining at home afterwards?'

'No, Daddy. I have to see someone in St Swithin's. About my destitutes. And as you know, I must be back at the hostel by ten.'

The dean twinkled. 'Perhaps you may find yourself invited to dine by one of the unattached housemen? I specifically ordered as many as could be spared from duty to support me in the Founders' Hall tonight. I know that Mr Havens and Mr Raffles will certainly be there. They are shortly coming up for better jobs.'

As Josephine handed a glass to her daughter, he decided, 'Perhaps you *could* pour me a gin and tonic, my dear. I believe a little lubrication has improved even the greatest orators, like Sir Winston Churchill. Lancelot won't be there, of course,' he continued shortly. 'Very uncivil of him to refuse. But I expect he would only have laughed in the wrong places, doubtless deliberately. The Matron of the Bertie Bunn will be presiding, the St Swithin's Matron – or Supreme Nursing Commander or whatever her new-fangled title is these days – being on holiday in Morocco. Morocco! We overtaxed and overworked consultants can hardly afford Minehead. If I weren't able to earn a few extra pence slaving away early mornings and late at night and entire weekends with our private beds in the Bertie Bunn, I don't know how we'd make ends meet at all. Have I time to run through my whole speech again?'

'No,' said his wife.

The three stepped into a still, clear, bright evening, almost as warm as midday. The dean lived in Lazar Row, one of the short alleys on the fringe of the City of London which so pleasantly lodge its minute nightly population. It had once contained the St Swithin's pesthouse, but now provided some redbrick Georgian dwellings for the more privileged of its consultants, among which the dean always succeeded in finding himself. Its convenience appealed to him, and so did the low rent. And being a man with a fond if erratic grasp on history, it pleased him to look through the bow-fronted parlour windows on an evening and imagine the shades of Mr Pepys or Dr Johnson or Mr Milton strolling their way home.

Round the corner, the new tower of St Swithin's burst from the City soil so richly fertilized with tradition. The old forecourt still separated the hospital from the road, to one side had been carefully preserved the Inigo Jones Founders' Hall and the garish Victorian chapel. The dean recalled that Mr Clapper had been campaigning vigorously for the demolition of both to make room for an adequate new incinerator and body store. 'Perhaps I should say a bit about euthanasia?' he mused. 'There seems to be a lot of it about this time of the year.'

'It would be much better if you told a few jokes,' his wife advised.

'I don't know any jokes. I don't seem to be the sort of person people tell jokes *to*,' he explained a little sadly.

'Some of the male nurses look dreadfully scruffy,' she remarked, observing the small crowd round the hall door.

'Scruffiness is the fashion these days,' said the dean disapprovingly. 'You can't tell some of them from the porters. Which reminds me, I experienced a most peculiar coincidence this evening. I was walking across the concourse in St Swithin's on my way home, when I ran into a porter who was the spit and image of that scamp Chipps, whom I expelled from the hospital after he behaved like a homicidal maniac in his surgery finals yesterday morning. Most strange. I suppose that unintelligent, feckless sort of face is common enough in the working classes. What's the matter, Faith?'

'Hay fever, Daddy. Did he say anything to you?'

'I've no idea. I just strode by. I've better things to do than chat to hospital porters. If young people *must* wear jeans, they should wear them with a decent crease down the front,' he declared, looking at the crowd with distaste. 'A great pity the nurses aren't still ordered to wear their uniforms for this occasion. Like with everything else these days, they're left to do as they please. The young ladies all sitting there with turned up tails to their caps reminded me of rows of pouter pigeons.'

'What's the matter, Faith?' asked her mother. 'You look worried.'

'It's just that I've got a strange feeling something might go wrong.'

'Rubbish,' laughed the dean. 'You've got stage fright, that's all. Nothing can possibly go wrong with the matron of the Bertie Bunn organizing the revels.'

They made their way among the crowd drifting into the main door of the hall. The dean always liked to reach the far platform through the seated audience, as impressively as possible.

# 11

There was another small, hardly noticeable doorway at the far end of the barn-like brick hall, where Pip was saying to Harold Sapworth, 'I can't go on.'

'Go on?'

'I said I can't.'

'Can't what?'

'Can't go on. Go on the stage,' Pip told him desperately.

'Go on?'

'Harold, for God's sake say something different.'

'Keep your hair on. I'm only trying to help.'

'I just peeped in there,' Pip glanced anxiously over the shoulder of his brown coat. 'Through the door there's a little stairway, with another door at the top. I pushed it open a bit. I could see the whole hall absolutely crammed to the rafters,' he gasped.

'Must be a strike blacking out the telly.'

'Almost the entire St Swithin's membership of ACHE should be there.' Pip rubbed his palms in gratification. 'It's quite amazing, even to me. I never imagined I'd get so many to turn up, just by buzzing round the hospital for one afternoon. I must have enormous powers of persuasion. Yet I'd never one inkling that I possessed them. Perhaps I ought to have taken up salesmanship for some drug company. I'd have made a fortune.'

'Have a drop of that whisky what you bought,' suggested Harold, producing a bottle from under his own brown coat.

'It seems to have gone down a bit,' Pip observed tartly.

'I've got the wind up, too.'

'Do you know, there's also a lot of junior nurses speckled about in their uniforms.' Pip took a swig. 'Which proves that even the nursing staff are solid with us against the private patients. It's odd, I never thought the nurses cared about the Bertram Bunn Wing one way or another. And the platform itself! That door up the stairs leads directly on to it. The whole stage is decked with lovely flowers, there's microphones and little gilt chairs all over the place.'

'Must be Mr Grout's doing.' Harold took a gulp of the whisky.

'I suppose when these hospital administrators decide to do something, they do it properly,' Pip agreed admiringly. 'I must revise my opinion of them. I thought Mr Grout and Mr Clapper only a pair of self-opinionated, self-satisfied, self-important, incompetent, overpaid cretins.'

Harold sucked the tip of his thumb. 'What are you going to say to the lads and lassies?'

'That's the trouble.' Pip suddenly turned gloomy. 'Faced with such a vast audience, I don't think I could physically open my mouth. It's very flattering that so many have come to hear me, and I expect they'll be wildly enthusiastic. But to tell the truth, I've never made a speech in my life. Not even at occasions like weddings or rugger club Saturday nights.'

'A bright bloke like you will think of something off the cuff,' Harold encouraged him. 'I remember once, seeing a stand-up comic in a club. Died the death, he did. Then he noticed one of our blokes sitting up front with a bit of black velvet. He started making jokes about race relations, and that. Soon had everyone rolling on the floor. It'll be the same with you.'

'If only I'd prepared a formal speech,' said Pip in anguish. 'Of course, I imagined after all you said, Harold, that only a couple of fellows would bother to turn up. I could give them a chat rather than a harangue. But now I know that I shall dry up. Everyone will hiss me, and even throw things. Tomorrow I'll have to resign as shop steward, and probably be sent to Coventry into the bargain.'

'Another bevvy?'

'Thanks.' Pip took the bottle. The clock on the Founders' Hall began to strike seven. 'If they do try and lynch me, Harold, use the rest of this stuff for setting the place on fire to cause a diversion.'

Pip went through the small door. Followed by Harold Sapworth, he climbed the steps inside as though ascending a gallows. At the top he paused, took a deep breath, and threw open the door leading on to the stage.

The St Swithin's Founders' Hall was lofty and oblong. Half a dozen tall deep-set windows stood along each wall, between them oak panelling encrusted in gilt with the names of hospital benefactors – City merchants and worthies from those centuries when ten pounds could buy remembrance to eternity. Portraits of past St Swithin's consultants, commissioned by the medical school, here and there gazed down with expressions of surpassing wisdom in gorgeous academic robes. The dean had planned his own, sagaciously contemplating a skull, a combination of Hamlet and Rodin's *The Thinker*, unaware of Sir Lancelot Spratt's widely expressed determination that he would countenance first an oil-painting of Dr Harvey Crippen. The portrait of Sir Bertram Bunn himself, pink-cheeked, generously moustached and paunched, frock-coated and gold watch-chained, ironically looked from the rear of the stage in moneyed affability.

As Pip stepped on to the platform the packed audience gave a thunderous burst of applause, with foot-stamping and one or two little cheers. Gratified if mystified, Pip stepped towards the geraniums and hydrangeas with a modest bow of acknowledgment. Then he noticed the dean taking the stage from the flight of steps leading down into the hall.

The dean halted. Pip faced him. The audience fell into an uneasy silence. The matron of the Bertram Bunn in her uniform, following the dean's wife and daughter up the steps, could be heard complaining piercingly, 'Haven't those porters got the platform ready yet? They grow lazier and lazier every day.'

'Hello,' said Pip to the dean. He gave a faint smile and a flutter of the fingers. 'Our paths do rather keep crossing, don't they?'

'Chipps! What's this?' hissed the dean. 'Get off this stage at once. And out of this hospital.'

Pip looked puzzled. 'But what are you doing at my meeting?'

'Your meeting? This is my meeting. I've spent all week getting ready for it.'

Pip shook his head. 'I'm afraid there's some mistake. You see, I booked the hall tonight for a branch meeting of ACHE. Mr Grout gave his permission. It was all arranged perfectly correctly. Through the usual channels.'

'I've had enough of your stupid practical jokes,' said the dean in suppressed fury. 'Get out this instant. Or I'll send for a couple of porters to throw you out.'

'They'd hardly do that,' Pip told him amiably. 'You see, I'm the porters' shop steward.'

The dean held a hand to his eyes. 'I'm dreaming. This is one of my nightmares when I've been foolish enough to indulge in the crackling off the pork. In a moment, I'll wake up beside Josephine with a nice hot cuppa ready in the Teasmade – '

'Pip!' came a screech from the matron. She pushed on to the stage, cap streamers flying. '*What* do you mean by this perfectly outrageous intrusion?'

The audience began to mutter and titter, shifting with embarrassment in their chairs. The unexpected drama had to them a straightforward plot. The dean was upbraiding one of the hospital porters, who seemed to be taking it with commendable cheerfulness. Meanwhile, the matron was having one of her turns.

'Oh, hello, Auntie Florrie.' Pip gave another smile and little wave. 'It's not an intrusion, honestly.' He nodded towards the audience. 'Those are all members of my union. I'm about to address them, as one of their duly appointed officials. It's democracy in action.'

'There's nothing democratic about this,' she told him hotly. 'It's the nurses' prizegiving.'

'Oh, really?' asked Pip with interest.

'Furthermore, you absolutely reek of drink.'

'Really, everyone is becoming over-excited,' said Josephine calmly, coming to the centre of the stage while the audience sat in open-mouthed confusion. 'It's quite obvious there's been a slight mistake. Mr Clapper booked the hall for the nurses' prizegiving. Mr Grout booked the hall for this young man to do whatever he wants to do in it. It's like on our last holiday in Ibiza, Lionel, when we had to muck in with that peculiar taxidermist couple from Scunthorpe.'

'Those bloody administrators,' exclaimed the dean angrily. 'They're all the same. If they'd existed in the Garden of Eden, the world today would be full of nothing but apples and serpents. Telephone them at once, Matron. I demand Mr Clapper or Mr Grout instantly, in person.'

'Not much hope of that,' Pip told him. 'They're all off home promptly at five. No overtime, see.'

'No wonder the country's in such a terrible state. Obviously, you'll have to give way, Chipps. I've no idea what you're doing in ACHE, or even in that coat. This is hardly the moment to sort out such complexities. Doubtless, it's another of your inane jokes. The nurses' prizegiving is infinitely more important than one of your seditious little union cabals. Besides, those are our flowers,' he pointed out.

'Don't worry, I shan't be unreasonable,' Pip told him calmly. 'Me and my friend –' He indicated Harold Sapworth, clutching the whisky bottle under his brown coat, nervously trying to creep unseen to the hall steps behind a fringe of palms in tubs. 'Will convene a meeting down in the hospital garage, or somewhere. I don't suppose more than half a dozen of this audience came to hear me, anyway.' The dean gave him a brisk satisfied nod. 'In a way, it's a relief. I don't think I could have brought myself to address such a mass of strange faces.'

'Public speaking is indeed an art,' the dean agreed with him. 'Given to only a few of us. It calls for considerable memory, concentration and practice.'

'You rehearse, do you?' Pip inquired. 'Not just get up and say whatever comes to mind?'

'Oh, dear me, no,' the dean told him condescendingly. 'I practise before a mirror every morning in the bathroom. The same pains were taken by such renowned orators as the late Lloyd George and the late Adolf Hitler.'

'I lack the gift,' Pip said unhappily. 'I lack the confidence.'

'I might be able to give you a lesson or two –'

The dean was brought back to reality by the slow handclap starting in the hall. He stepped decisively to the microphone amid the geraniums. 'Ladies and gentlemen. I must apologize for a slight technical hitch. The porter is now about to leave the stage.'

'Pip –' The dean spun round. Faith had pushed between her mother and the matron. 'Don't budge, Pip, love. You were here first.' She threw herself into his brown-coated arms.

The dean held his hand over his eyes again. 'Yes, it is a dream. Have I got my clothes on?' He glanced down. 'They'll fly off in a minute. They always do. I shall be standing stark naked before the entire nursing staff of St Swithin's. I'm repeatedly getting this dream. I really must see Dr Bonaccord just as soon as I wake up.'

'Don't give in, lovey,' urged Faith, as the audience began to stir with excitement. 'Stand by your principles. If you let them trample all over you about this meeting, it'll be a long time before you get back either your credibility or your self-respect. You stay,' she advised firmly.

'You're absolutely right,' Pip exclaimed. 'It's the old boxing-match again, which my friend Harold keeps going on about.' He nodded towards Harold Sapworth, who was trying to squeeze between the matron and a pedestalled bust of Galen. 'Drop your guard once, and the bosses will clout you before you can say Keir Hardie. I won't take more than a couple of minutes,' he told the dean accommodatingly. 'Then you can hand out all those certificates and volumes of Dickens and forget I was ever in the way.'

'You will do nothing of the kind,' the dean returned. 'And put down my daughter at once. You don't even know her.'

'Stick to your guns, Pip,' whispered Faith. 'And open fire.'

Pip grasped the microphone from the dean. 'I hereby declare this branch meeting of the Amalgamated Confederation of Hospital Employees well and truly open.'

The audience broke into loud clapping.

'Mass hysteria,' muttered the dean. 'Good God.'

He grabbed Pip by the arm. Instantly, the audience booed and hissed. The dean stared. Like Brutus, he discovered with dismay the fickleness and treachery of any mob. He sank ingloriously on to a gilt chair. He was flanked on one side by the matron, who he noticed was scowling fiercely. And on the other by his wife, who seemed to be enjoying it all.

'Ladies and gentlemen,' said Pip.

He stopped. The hall sat in utter, expectant and titillated silence. He could not think what to say next.

'Ladies and gentlemen,' he repeated.

Another pause. He heard inauspicious shuffling and coughs. Then occurred the most meaningful event of his life to date. Standing beside him, Faith slipped her hand in his.

'Brothers and sisters, comrades in the endless battle against death and disease in St Swithin's.' His voice rang through the hall. 'You may reject me as an intruder in your revels. But you must accept me as an intruder in your consciences. I have a message, which is simple and unshakeable. In this hospital, every one of us – doctors, nurses, porters, ambulance drivers, telephonists, cooks and cleaners, have three purposes which outshine all others in our working days. One, to keep the patients alive. Two, getting them better. Three, making them happy. I assure you that sentiment exists as strongly in the porters' room down in the basement as in the consultants' mess which occupies most of the top floor.'

There was a burst of clapping, spiced with cheers.

'But what *is* St Swithin's? To which we give our energies, our sentiments, sometimes our whole lives? I'll tell you what it is – a "prole hospital". Where people are crowded together in bleak wards, strictly disciplined, fed on plain food, demonstrated upon to students – patients both awake and unconscious, their insides as well as their outsides – cut off from their friends, without the freedom even of choosing their own channel on the telly. Besides, the service lift is an utter disgrace,' he remembered. 'But those better-off patients who have in their pockets the golden key to the Bertram Bunn Wing –'

He was halted by a growl of approval swelling to a roar, a cheer on which claps were now the decoration. The nurses' prizegiving had become far more entertaining than everyone had steeled themselves for.

'I knew it was mass hysteria,' frowned the dean. 'Even the nurses have caught it. It's like a night out with a bunch of lemmings. Dr Bonaccord's going to have his work cut out for months.'

'Comrades in humanity,' Pip declaimed. 'What is the Bertram Bunn Wing? An obnoxious obscenity.'

'Stop!' cried the matron, jumping from her gilt chair.

'Sorry, Auntie Florrie.' Pip blinked at her. 'Have I said something rude?'

'Get off this stage at once. You have already insulted me personally once today. I will not now have everything I've worked for subjected to insults derived from warped class-consciousness.'

'Sit down,' shouted several voices from the audience.

'Shut up,' the matron snapped back. She turned to Pip. She was pink and quivering, like the chef's famous salmon mousse on its way to one of her patients. 'Fortunately, your perverse opinions are of monumental inconsequence. I advise you to get out of this hall at once and continue from a soapbox at the nearest street corner.'

'And that's your last word, Auntie?'

'Emphatically. I shall not address another to you as long as I live.'

Pip turned back to the microphone. 'Comrades against suffering. I now relinquish the floor to the dean. Thank you for listening to the single, simple point I called this meeting to make. Who are the paid-up members of ACHE?' A few hands were raised, Harold Sapworth's with an empty bottle. 'Brothers, the Bertram Bunn is blacked. As far as the private patients are concerned, from now we're on strike.'

For the second time that day, Pip excited a burst of clapping from an admiring female, this time the dean's daughter.

# 12

Just before nine on the following sunny morning, Sir Lancelot Spratt stepped through the automatic glass doors into the lobby of the Bertram Bunn Wing.

'Thank God for that,' he muttered. The piped music had stopped. The suggestion of the East was stronger, because the air was hotter. The air conditioning had failed, Sir Lancelot decided. Well, he never liked its deadening year-old sameness, anyway.

His eye fell on the white plastic counter. The two porters and the receptionist were late coming on duty. There seemed fewer people about than usual, just one voluminously black-gowned family sitting on the floor chewing nuts.

'Lancelot.' The matron appeared instantly, pink-faced and fiery-eyed at the door of her office.

'This morning I'm somewhat preoccupied,' he told her firmly.

'*You*'re preoccupied! We're all preoccupied. Revolution has broken out.'

'I must see Miss Bristols directly, to inform her that the X-rays are clear. I shall be operating on her breast this afternoon.'

'You won't. Not on any part of Miss Bristols. Nor of anyone else. We're in the grip of anarchy. The porters and people are on strike.'

'Really?' murmured Sir Lancelot. 'A local outbreak of the English disease? It is of course a form of national hysteria, like the mass flagellants of Central Europe in the fourteenth century.'

'That may well be the case,' she snapped at him. 'But my patients haven't had any breakfast.'

'My patients in St Swithin's have had a very good breakfast of sausage and bacon.'

'Naturally. The blockade is directed only against the hospital's private patients. The main switchboard is even refusing to put through their phone calls. Some of my stockbroker patients are becoming very distressed. Envy, malice and resentment! *Those* are the diseases these shirkers are suffering from.' She shuddered. 'Little could I have imagined this situation, when I first dedicated myself to nursing. Haven't you seen the morning papers?'

'I have only got back to London. I had to go fishing in Berkshire yesterday evening, to avoid attending the nurses' prizegiving.'

'Haven't you even seen the pickets?' she demanded angrily. 'Intimidating peaceable people outside our front entrance?'

'I saw only one of the mortuary porters, Forfar McBridie. He was wearing the kilt, plaid, sporran, bonnet and so on, a skean-dhu stuck in one of his tartan socks and a sprig of white heather in the other. He was assuredly carrying a placard.'

'What did it say?'

' "It's Scotland's Oil." They are an enviably single-minded race. But what have the porters gone on strike about?' Sir Lancelot asked with interest. 'The only industrial discontent to reach my ears was the lack of a darts board down in their room.'

'Nothing. They are striking because the dunderheads do absolutely everything my nephew Pip tells them. He's their shop steward.'

Sir Lancelot paused, stroking his beard. 'I am a little lost.'

'He got a job as a porter, when you threw him out of the hospital on Tuesday. It's all your fault,' she ended bitterly.

'Hardly. The dean threw the unfortunate young man out, not I. Quite possibly, I should have passed him. Once I had overcome my reasonable irritation at his commencing the examination of his first patient by attempting to eviscerate the eye-socket.'

'Then you must get the dean to reinstate him at once.'

'I can hardly intervene in the internal affairs of the medical school. There the dean reigns supreme. Wouldn't there be more point in your talking to Pip as a Dutch Auntie? Tell him to call his little strike off again.'

'I refuse to utter another word to Pip in this world.'

'In which case, I can't see more chance of resolving the situation than between a couple of chimpanzees fighting over a bunch of bananas.'

'You are not being in the slightest helpful,' she told him, slamming the door.

Sir Lancelot shrugged his broad shoulders and continued across the patterned mosaic floor of the lobby. He was unwarmed by the matron's red-hot indignation. He suspected it was all some prank hatched in the residents' bar. He reached the lift as the doors slid open. The dean stepped out, walking straight past him.

'I say, Dean – '

'The dean stopped. He stared at Sir Lancelot without recognition, blinking behind his large round glasses.

'Dean! It's Lancelot. Wake up.'

The dean jumped, as Sir Lancelot gave a sharp pinch to his biceps. 'Ah, yes. Good morning.'

'The matron would appear to be having trouble with her industrial relations.'

'The apocalypse is upon us. As from yesterday evening.'

'Isn't everyone making heavy weather of a sportive little breeze?' Sir Lancelot asked a little irritably. 'It's only another manifestation of that harebrained Chipps' twisted sense of humour.'

The dean shuddered. 'You are talking of my son-in-law.'

Sir Lancelot stared. 'I never heard that Faith was even contemplating marriage.'

'Neither did I. But apparently she and this medical Mad Hatter are joined in what they call an "open marriage". I've no idea what that means. It sounds like some sort of public conveyance.'

'They might have invited me,' Sir Lancelot grumbled. 'I've known Faith since the day she was delivered, up in the old maternity ward.'

The dean gave a laugh sounding like interference on the radio. 'How delightfully old-fashioned you are. There was no ceremony. Not so much as going to the post office and buying a dog licence. Apparently you become married these days by saying so. You "shack up" together. I don't know what that means, either. It sounds like something you do in the garden. Mind, I suppose it saves all that fuss with clergymen and organists, and the considerable expense to which the bride's father is, to my mind, quite unreasonably committed by some obscure tradition. With my elder daughter, the florists' bills alone – '

'This too is only some juvenile foolishness,' Sir Lancelot comforted him brusquely. 'Marriage these days is simply another amusement which has come within the economic grasp of the young, like holidays abroad and fast motor cars. It is old fogeys like us, who after so many years upon earth, come to take both marriage and death rather seriously.'

'They flaunt it,' the dean objected. 'In my face. If I had a mistress I'd keep pretty quiet about her, believe you me. I think Faith should see a psychiatrist. I've been looking everywhere for Dr Bonaccord.'

'But the nuptial knot is loose. It may vanish once the rush of blood is past. Like an absorbable ligature.'

The dean shook his head gloomily. 'I shall emigrate. To a leprosy practice, like Dr Schweitzer. I shall spend the fag-end of my life sitting in some steamy jungle contemplating the wrongs which the world has done me.'

'In the meantime, hadn't you better do something to see the private patients get some breakfast?'

'I suppose someone had better galvanize that pompous bungler Clapper. I doubt if he has even noticed that the whole hospital is falling about our ears.'

The dean maligned the hospital administrator. A few minutes later he found Mr Clapper with Mr Grout in his spacious first-floor office in St Swithin's, eyeing the front pages of the morning papers spread all over his desk, and wearing the expression of a cat who is not certain whether the noise it hears is mice or a large dog.

'We have had quite a "Press" as the expression goes, Sir Lionel,' he told the dean. 'We're on all the front pages.'

'If only I hadn't asked that colitic gossip writer,' the dean said bitterly. 'The story got round Fleet Street in a flash. It's like having one's family quarrels paraded to titillate the whole country over its breakfast.'

'One big, efficient and above all happy family,' remarked Mr Clapper, sitting back with his hands folded across his stomach. 'That is the administrator's duty, to create it from his hospital staff. Don't I always say so, Mr Grout?'

'Yes, Mr Clapper,' said the junior administrator, respectfully at his side.

'No easy task, I grant you. A hospital employs people of vastly differing skills, intelligence, training, education, traditions, ethics, outlooks and even tastes in canteen nourishment. Odd, how doctors don't eat curry. It is a task demanding the utmost skill and tact, to avoid conflict between one group and another. One must expect occasionally some disruption.

'Yes, but how are you going to settle it?' demanded the dean.

'We are putting our minds to it. Aren't we, Mr Grout?'

'Yes, Mr Clapper.'

'Meanwhile, the newspapers make us look a bunch of fools.' The dean threw a lordly glance at one of the tabloids, its headline announcing,

MATRON BRENDA!

The front page was mostly filled with a photograph of Brenda Bristols in her plungy nightdress, leaning over a goggle-eyed Lord Hopcroft as she handed him a glass of water in bed. The story beneath read,

*Brenda Bristols and other pampered patients in St Swithin's Hospital private wing will wake to a rude shock this morning. Their domestic staff are on strike. No one will serve their gourmet meals, sweep their expensive rooms or even push them into the operating theatre. It's going to be do-it-yourself treatment day. Patients well enough are learning to tend their sicker companions. 'I'm going to love it,' says Brenda, in for minor surgery. 'I always intended to be a nurse.'*

The dean snorted. 'This frivolous woman is turning the whole thing into a publicity stunt. Sir Lancelot really ought to control his patients better. She could at least have worn a dressing-gown.'

'It's really most irregular,' complained Mr Clapper. 'All this is covered by Circular HM bracket fifty-six bracket fifty-eight, Information to Press about Condition of Patients.'

Below was a picture of Pip and Faith, looking self-conscious outside the St Swithin's main door.

*Firebrand union leader "Pip" Chipps and girlfriend Faith on the picket line*, the dean read with an expressionless face. *Pip is a former medical student, Faith the daughter of St Swithin's medical school Dean Sir Lionel Lychfield. 'It's against natural justice, having*

*one ward for the rich, another for the poor,' Pip said. Faith added, 'Daddy always encouraged me to have an independent mind.'*

'The British Press is incurably irresponsible,' he complained. 'There's not a word about the hospital's side of the case.'

'I shall hold a press conference,' Mr Clapper decided. 'That is a procedure allowed for under official regulations – Ministry Circulars RHB bracket fifty-two bracket eighteen and HNC bracket fifty-two seventeen, as I remember. We will sit behind large cards with our names and functions – Mr Clapper, Senior Hospital Administrator, that sort of thing. We are authorized to provide reasonable refreshment, I think coffee and biscuits rather than whisky, Mr Grout. We can hold it in the Founders' Hall, we might as well get full use from the flowers provided for last night. We shall be quoted in the papers, we shall be heard on the radio, we shall be seen on the telly.' He squared his shoulders. 'My wife and daughters will be very pleased.'

'I've put five girls to answer all Press inquiries on the telephone, Mr Clapper,' said Mr Grout, as his superior nodded approval. 'Though the papers seem mainly interested in knowing when the most famous pair in the country are going to be reshaped.'

'Pair of what?' asked Mr Clapper.

'It's something to do with Brenda Bristols,' Mr Grout explained tactfully. 'The newspapers do rather concentrate on people's looks.'

'Appearances are false,' pronounced Mr Clapper.

'Brenda Bristols' aren't,' said Mr Grout.

'You may leave the dean and myself in conference, Mr Grout,' said Mr Clapper severely.

'It won't be the slightest use meeting the Press,' the dean told Mr Clapper as his office door closed. 'Reporters don't like being told they've got hold of the wrong end of the stick, no more than we doctors do. We'll just have to stand shoulder to shoulder in the pillory, putting on a bold face for them to throw rotten eggs at. We'll have to hope that the public will forget this stupid incident in a day or two, just as they forget absolutely everything else they read in the newspapers, once they've gone to wrap chips or been put to some other use.'

'Why, there's a photograph of me,' exclaimed Mr Clapper, opening the pages. 'It was the one taken at the last Hospital Administrators *v.* Prison Governors golf match. My wife and daughters will be most interested.' He produced a large pair of scissors and started carefully cutting it out. 'You think the strike will be over in a few days, then?' he asked, not looking up.

'If I play my cards right. I am going to be extremely crafty.' The dean tapped his nose with his forefinger. 'I can be crafty when necessary. I have to be, in order to keep one jump ahead of my perfidious students. This fellow Chipps has an Achilles' heel in which sits a Trojan Horse. My daughter Faith.'

'Of course, Sir Lionel. One word from you, she'll mend her ways and send this Chipps packing.'

'One must be realistic,' the dean admitted. 'Daughters do not show a proper respect for their fathers' wishes any more. But I shall appeal to her intelligence and her sense of reason, of fairness, of rectitude. These are qualities which she enjoys richly. After all, she *is* my daughter.'

The desk telephone buzzed. 'Excuse me,' said Mr Clapper. 'Hello? You have a German doctor? What German doctor? Oh, of philosophy. Send the Kraut to Mr Grout. I'm far too busy.'

'As Faith is undoubtedly somewhere about the hospital with her inamorato,' the dean continued eagerly as Mr Clapper replaced the telephone, 'I shall tackle her forthwith. I'm sure I can make her see the light. Otherwise, I shall simply have to throw the poor child to Dr Bonaccord.'

He left the office with a resolute step.

# 13

Outside Mr Clapper's door was waiting a small, thin, brown man in a towelling hospital dressing-gown. He immediately grasped the dean by his lapels and said desperately, 'Sir Lionel Lychfield... I know you. I've seen you in the ward. Help me, I beseech you. I must get out of here at once.'

The dean staggered back, alarmed. 'Don't tell me the patients are on strike, too?'

'I am not his patient. I am his brother-in-law.'

'I don't think I entirely follow,' said the dean confusedly.

'Professor Ding's. From Shanka. He is going to take my heart out and put in some total stranger's.'

'Oh, yes, I remember now. He's here on an exchange professorship arranged by the Ministry of Overseas Development. An extremely worthy idea for breaking down tensions in Brixton and such places. He's only doing it for your own good,' the dean comforted the patient, trying to disentangle his fingers.

'He is doing it for a fat pension from the crook who runs our country,' the man said bitterly. 'My heart is absolutely tip-top. I have bad feet, but my brother-in-law isn't interested in operating on feet, which have little glamour.'

'If you have any complaint whatever about your treatment,' the dean told him, freeing himself, 'you need have no fear that it will go unheard. As long as it's well-grounded, efficient action will most certainly be taken on your behalf.'

'Ah! Good!' The man's face suffused with joy. 'I knew you were a good fellow. Wisdom and benevolence flash from your eyes as sunlight from precious jewels.'

'Thank you.'

'My relief is indeed heartfelt. How do I go about making use of this most welcome information?'

'You are in a National Health Service Hospital, so you can enjoy all the benefits of our National Health Service administration. Exactly as if you had the advantage to be born a British subject,' the dean explained. 'A personage has been created exactly for your purposes. His title is the "Health Commissioner", though the public always refer to him as the "Ombudsman".'

"Ombudsman",' repeated the patient slowly. 'Please, Sir Lionel, when can I find this powerful individual in the hospital?'

'Oh, he isn't in the hospital.' The dean gave an amused glance. 'I don't know where he is, exactly. I suppose you could try Whitehall. But his location is immaterial, because of course all complaints must be made in writing. Mr Clapper in this office will certainly know the correct procedure.' He indicated the door behind him. 'You should certainly get a reply one way or another within six months to a year.

'But in six months I shall be dead and buried,' the man said, aghast. 'With somebody else's heart inside me, too.'

'Well, that's your problem, I suppose. Will you excuse me? I've an urgent meeting in the basement.'

The patient grasped the dean's lapels again. 'But, Sir Lionel – don't you understand? Wherever this functionary exists, I must have him release me from the hospital immediately.'

'There is nothing whatever to stop you discharging yourself whenever you feel inclined,' the dean told him testily, trying to dislodge the fingers again. 'This is St Swithin's, not Wormwood Scrubs.'

'Ah, there you is, my old china – !' A voice came booming down the corridor. 'You sure got me worried.'

The huge jovial figure of Professor Ding approached rapidly. His patient grasped the dean more firmly, making whimpering noises.

'For just a minute you had me thinking that you was getting scared and doing the bunk before your life-saving operation. Sir Lionel Lychfield,

I presume?' He laughed loudly, shaking the dean's hand powerfully while clasping his diminutive patient firmly round the shoulders. 'This one, he mighty nervous. I keep telling him, "Don't you quake so, sonny, this operation past the experimental stage, just routine, like having your tonsils out." '

'Most certainly great strides have been made in the technique of transplant surgery,' the dean nodded agreement.

'Nothing to it. We just waiting for some stupid bugger crash his car, come into hospital with the old heart still going pit-a-pat, but no breathing, no brain, no nothing, we plug him on to the old respirator, and we say, "Okay, count down to blast off", then we sharpen up the old knife and we dig in.' He squeezed the patient fondly, making him gurgle. 'Simple as eating your Sunday dinner.'

'You are in very good hands,' the dean explained patiently to the little man, still pulling at his fingers. 'I understood from the Ministry of Overseas Development that Professor Ding has an enormous reputation in your own country.'

'As a witch doctor,' said the patient.

Professor Ding patted him several times on the back, making his jaw wobble. 'This ignorant sod don't know which doctor is which doctor,' he said. 'Joke, hey?' He laughed, but not as loud as usual. 'Cummon, sonny boy. You and me gonna play lots more nice games of Scrabble, hey?' He gave his patient a jerk, ripping him from the dean's lapels. 'We play Scrabble till that unknown benefactor of humanity goes and wipes his four litre sports job along a brick wall, hey?'

The dean hurried away in the direction of the stairs, reflecting on the tenderness of African surgical professors, who so considerately calmed their patients' preoperative nerves by playing cards with them. He could hardly imagine Sir Lancelot making up a four at bridge with a gastrectomy, a cholecystectomy and some piles.

The St Swithin's concourse downstairs looked much as usual. Nobody seemed to be taking much notice of a single porter in his brown coat standing with a placard saying BACK ACHE. Through the front door, the dean could see a television camera with its crew, and the kilted Forfar McBridie marching up and down for them playing the bagpipes.

The dean turned towards the steps leading into the basement. He saw his first difficulty as prizing Faith away from the side of Pip. Possibly he would have to utter some white lie, like her mother having broken a leg. But this was spared him by Faith herself hurrying upstairs. 'Daddy,' she said at once. 'I want to have a very serious word with you.'

The dean invited her into the staff canteen behind the lifts for a cup of coffee.

'Daddy,' said Faith, sipping from her white plastic beaker as they took a table in one corner. 'You have been very, very naughty.'

'Me?' returned her father indignantly. 'When I have been humiliated before our entire complement of student nurses by my own daughter, who openly connives with this pint-sized Lenin to inflict starvation upon my patients –'

She laid a finger softly on his lips. 'Daddy, you are suffering from hubris.'

'You make it sound like a particularly unpleasant disease, and I am not suffering from anything of the kind.'

'Yes, you are,' she said quietly. 'You and all the doctors at St Swithin's. The sorrow is that you don't know you've got it. And as you always say, Daddy, it's the patient who makes his disease fatal, by overlooking it. I worry about you, honestly I do.' She looked at him wide-eyed. 'You forget that the hospital care of sick people is a team effort –'

'Of course I don't. I tell the students exactly that every year in my inaugural lecture. Some of the old hands know it well, and utter groans at that juncture.'

'But a team effort of the humblest as well as the highest,' she persisted softly. 'A hospital can't work without consultants. But it can't work without porters or laundry workers or cleaners, either.'

'Exactly. The difference is, my dear,' he told her tartly, 'that my importance is apparent when I start work. Theirs only when they stop.'

Faith considered this. 'I don't think that alters the principle. Anyway, Pip doesn't see it that way. He wants you to arrange for representatives of these workers to have a seat on the council which runs St Swithin's. Then he'll call off the strike.'

'Outrageous! Am I to argue about such matters as the provision of a new electroencephalograph, or even of a place to park my car, with one of the hospital *porters*?' he asked contemptuously.

'Pip says that's what happens in Russia,' she told him calmly. 'All the health service workers have been in the same union for years. Including the doctors. And everyone knows that Russian medicine is among the best in the world.'

'I don't care if Russian doctors operate to the sound of balalaikas and have snow on their rubber boots. Here we've still got the shreds of democracy. Which means that I give the orders and the porters carry them out.' The dean folded his arms decisively.

Faith sighed. 'Well, Daddy, those are Pip's conditions for calling off the strike. Until they're met, I'm afraid you won't be able to use the Bertie Bunn for making more shekels from sheikhs. But that's the wrong currency, isn't it?'

'If Pip Chipps takes my advice, he'll hop on the next train home to Somerset. These porters will soon tumble to it, that he's simply leading them a dance to satisfy his own abnormal sense of humour. I shouldn't like to be in his shoes then. Pretty tough-looking eggs, some of the porters. Criminal records, too, I shouldn't doubt.'

'Please don't delude yourself, Daddy. We've no blacklegs and no scabs.'

'When I started medicine, a blackleg was an advanced form of gas gangrene, and a scab was something you got from chicken-pox. Now they mean anyone who values human life above union solidarity.'

'I know you feel frustrated over the trade unions, like many of your class,' she told him patiently. 'But you must accept modern life as it is.'

'Yes. With everyone doing exactly what they like, not giving a thought to the convenience or comfort of their fellow-beings. And the worst offenders of all are governments.'

Faith stood up. 'I must rush now. I've got a meeting of the strike committee. If you want to surrender, you've only to phone down to the porters' room.'

The dean banged the pink formica top of the table. 'We shall never surrender,' he declared stoutly. 'We shall fight at the bedsides, we shall fight on the landings, we shall fight in the filing departments and in the stores, we shall fight in the halls. We shall defend our hospital, whatever the cost may be. And furthermore, you stupid little girl,' he ended, losing his temper, 'all your lecherous lunatic's former student friends will give exactly that answer when I appeal to their common sense to chuck him out neck and crop.'

She left her father scowling into the dregs of his coffee. His diplomatic offensive seemed to have crumbled under her counter-attack. He would charge upon a more vulnerable flank.

# 14

'Look out, here comes trouble.' Tony Havens quickly emptied his pint of beer, set the mug down on the counter of the residents' bar and stood with his back to it. 'It's the dean,' he explained, nodding towards the door.

Hugo Raffles followed his companion's action promptly. 'He must have come to shut the place down,' he suggested gloomily.

'I can't think of any other reason. I've never seen the old buzzard in here all my days at St Swithin's.'

'Perhaps he's come to buy drinks all round?'

'You're more likely to get a fart out of a corpse.'

A hush fell upon the score or so young men and women gathered in the bar just before lunchtime that same day. Darts players became immobilized statues, billiards players froze at their cues, the fruit machine clicked into silence. 'He's smiling,' whispered Hugo urgently.

'At us,' agreed Tony, eyebrows raised.

'Perhaps he's drunk?'

'Or the strike's unhinged his mind. He seems to have taken it rather seriously. He's been going about all morning as though he was on the operating list for extramural cephalectomy.' He made a gesture across his throat.

'We'd better talk earnestly about medicine,' said Hugo, as the dean approached their corner.

Tony Havens nodded. 'It is very important to distinguish between Kleinfelter's syndrome and Turner's syndrome,' he observed loudly. 'Kleinfelter's has forty-seven chromosomes with an XXY constitution, but Turner's has of course forty-five chromosomes with an XO constitution.

Good morning, sir,' he broke off in surprise, as the dean appeared in front of his nose. 'This is an unexpected pleasure.'

'Ah… Havens… Raffles…care for a…er, jar?'

'That's extremely kind of you, sir.' Tony hid an intense curiosity over what was up. 'Neither of us is working this afternoon, and we are of course very conscious of your disapproval towards housemen who take the smallest sip while on call. I'm attending a refresher course – that's work, naturally, sir,' he added hastily, 'but only sort of sitting down-work.'

The dean smiled more widely. 'I'm sure you hard-pressed residents need to enjoy a relaxing drink once you have a few minutes' opportunity. Barman, two half-pints, please,' he ordered. 'I'll have a small sherry. I hear the Cyprus sort is excellent value for money. Chipps was a particular pal of you two, I believe?'

'We mucked in together a good deal as students,' Tony agreed.

'Mucked in,' repeated the dean, nodding thoughtfully. 'Well, I don't know who put up the idea to him of becoming a porter. Possibly it was some practical joke.' The pair looked innocent. The dean continued smiling. 'Naturally, I can take a joke. Eh? Havens? Raffles?'

'Renowned for it in the hospital, sir,' Hugo told him.

'Bung…er, ho.' The dean sipped his sherry. 'But it would seem that the joke has gone wrong. Or Chipps has gone wrong. The strain of the sudden social descent has afflicted him with paranoia. He was always most unstable mentally, as I'm sure you'll agree?' They nodded heartily. 'So his persecution mania drives him to organizing this ridiculous strike against his old friends and colleagues. The only result is getting our dear old hospital a bad name, pictures of half-naked actresses in the Press, that sort of thing.'

'The patients started pulling our legs as soon as they got their morning papers,' Tony told him.

'Not only the hospital but we consultants individually are losing our patients' good money – I mean good will. Obviously, this neurotic Napoleon downstairs would never listen to me. But you're his old friends. For the sake of St Swithin's, can't you persuade him to call it off?'

The pair exchanged glances. 'Pip's a pretty determined sort of chap, sir.'

'You mean, you don't want to appear as – er, dean's narks?'

'I think we'd just prefer to keep clear of someone else's row, sir.'

'But supposing I was able – Good God, have you finished a whole half pint already? Supposing I was able to make it worth your while?' The dean's smile developed an oily surface. 'Your jobs at St Swithin's end with the present month, remember. Doubtless you will be seeking posts more senior?'

'Not in St Swithin's, sir,' Hugo told him. 'It's this strike which finally made up our minds, as it happens. Private practice in Britain could be for the chop. We're emigrating.'

'So much the better.' The dean rubbed his hands slowly together. 'This very morning's post brought an inquiry for some rising young surgeon and anaesthetist to make a career at a privately run medical centre in Las Vegas, a town I understand to be a lively little place. The emoluments are so enormous that for a moment I considered working at both posts myself. There is also provided a ranch-type house, or house-type ranch, I forget which.'

'Car?' asked Hugo.

'Unfortunately no. Only the helicopter. I would just add that the appointment is entirely in my hands.'

The three fell silent. Tony and Hugo slowly put down their glasses. The dean remained smiling and rubbing his hands. 'I think you will find your friend in the basement,' he suggested. 'He seems to prefer commanding operations from underground, as Herr Hitler in his final stages.'

A few minutes later, Tony and Hugo were pushing open the door of the smoky porters' room. Several dozen men in unbuttoned brown coats were as usual lounging about the benches. One or two were listening without much interest to Pip, who was orating standing among copies of the morning's papers, Faith taking down his words in a large notebook. He broke off at once, striding to the door bright-eyed, brown coat flapping.

'An enormous success, isn't it?' he greeted his two friends. 'Meet the strike committee – Harold there, my left-hand man, and Faith my right-hand one. Without her,' he explained, slipping an arm tenderly round her shoulders, 'I should never have found this new determination to stand up to the people who've been pushing me about for years.'

'The strike is one hundred per cent solid,' said Harold Sapworth. 'At this moment of time, there's no possibility of a sell out, none whatever. The lads regret the inconvenience to the public, but someone's got to get hurt. We're ready at any time to meet with anyone who's going to talk sense.'

'Oh, Harold, do try to stop talking like a trade union leader on television,' Faith told him wearily.

'Power!' Pip slapped fist into palm. 'I have rediscovered the most powerful weapon of the century – organized workers. We are more powerful than any Army,' he declaimed, arms wide apart, turning to the rest of the room. 'An Army can only shoot us, thus getting a terribly bad Press all round the world. Moreover, Brothers, willing workers follow their leaders more blindly than any troops the most inspiring of military commanders.' The audience on the benches went on reading and playing cards, giving Tony and Hugo the impression of having heard it all before. 'Modern civilization has played into our hands by its very complexity. Even the means of securing such basic necessities of life as light and heat, food and water, have become unbelievably intricate since the days of candles and logs, cabbage-patches and wells. A few strategically placed workers can bring any community to its knees in a matter of days, even hours.'

Pip stopped, chin tipped towards the ceiling.

'Pip, don't you think you should have a word with Dr Bonaccord?' suggested Hugo seriously. 'It's his afternoon for behaviour therapy.'

'On the contrary, I have discovered my normal self. All my life I've been inhibited, frustrated, unaggressive. Faith has been my psychiatrist.' He embraced her again. 'She rubbed my lamp and the genie came out.'

'How vulgar,' murmured Hugo.

'And this gift for oratory. I never knew I possessed it. It's quite frightening how I can sway my audiences. I suppose Trotsky would have found the same, if he'd started addressing a nurses' prizegiving.'

'It's wonderful how Pip's become famous overnight from Land's End to John o' Groats,' said Faith admiringly.

'He could have achieved that by chucking a bomb at the Queen,' remarked Tony.

'Do I detect a certain hostility?' asked Pip, sounding hurt.

'You do. We think this strike is bloody cruel. It's against sick people.'

Pip looked aghast. 'There's nothing in the slightest cruel about us. Is there, Faith? We're only striking against the consultant capitalists. If sick people happen to be involved, it means that our industrial action must be settled all the sooner. A blitzkrieg does far less damage and kills far fewer people than something like the Somme.'

'Look, Pip –' Tony had reeled back, hand to forehead. 'Come up to the bar and have a drink.'

'A porter?' Pip grinned, flapping his brown coat with both hands. 'I won't embarrass you.'

'You became a porter for a joke. Right? To get your own back on the dean. Right? Well, the joke's over.'

'The dean threw me out.'

'The dean's thrown hundreds of students out. But they didn't take their revenge by wrecking the work and reputation of the hospital.'

'With which we are getting just the teeniest, weeniest bit fed up, dear boy,' Hugo told him.

Pip stuck both fists deep into his brown coat pockets. 'I hadn't thought of it like that,' he admitted solemnly. 'Am I really damaging the hospital's reputation?' They both nodded forcefully. 'I shouldn't care for that. After all, I'm part of St Swithin's, as much as ever.'

'That's more the way to talk,' said Tony warmly. 'And I'm sure you don't really want to antagonize old pals like us, who've helped you over the years. We'd even have got you through your finals, if only you'd poked the other eye.'

'That's true,' Pip agreed. 'You two had rather dropped out of my mind, with all the excitement.'

'So why not say, "It's been a big giggle, a great gas, but enough's enough"?'

'Who put you two up to this?' Faith asked crisply, snapping shut her notebook. 'My father, I suppose?'

She stared at Tony so knowingly, he could only reply evasively, 'We agreed to do it in Pip's own interest.'

'You didn't. My father mentioned to me over coffee this morning something about appealing to your better nature. Knowing my father and his students better than he thinks,' she continued evenly, 'I realized that he really meant he was going to bribe you. How much?'

'Is this true?' demanded Pip.

'Of course he didn't bribe us,' Tony replied indignantly. 'He merely agreed to help both of us to practise in Las Vegas.'

'Where everyone develops tennis-elbow from shaking hands with one-armed bandits,' Hugo added.

'You *were* bribed,' said Pip severely.

'Not really,' Hugo told him languidly. 'We're emigrating anyway.'

'You're not,' said Pip. 'You've just given me an absolutely brilliant idea. That'll be the next plank in my platform. It's barefaced robbery, newly qualified doctors walking off with an education obtained at the expense of the British taxpayer. I bet even ladies in Tory hats would agree with that. After all, it's mostly their taxes. Once we stop medical emigration, all our problems will be over. We can reduce doctors' salaries, finish private practice and at last have the National Health Service adequately financed and fully manned. The doctors will lose their single weapon in the fight. So simple.'

'How are you going to stop us going?' Tony asked defiantly.

'Easy. They manage it in Russia. As we're an island, there's no need for minefields. Medically qualified Channel swimmers I think would be a negligible problem.'

'You *are* mad,' he asserted. 'That's just not on. This isn't the Soviet Union. It isn't even Yugoslavia. It's Britain. And you can't interfere with the liberty of the individual.'

'Oh, individual liberty,' Pip said impatiently. 'That's got a cash value, like everything else. What sort of individual freedom can the workers of Britain afford? Not much. Think of all the places the capitalists can walk into without a second thought – hotels, restaurants, the Royal Enclosure at Ascot, the pavilion at Lord's, first-class carriages on the trains. I'm amazed the railwaymen's union haven't put a stop to that one. The workers are permanently barred from these places, because they haven't the money in their pockets, that's all.'

'We only ask for a fair and just settlement,' put in Harold Sapworth, who seemed not to be following the conversation.

Pip slapped fist into palm again. 'Faith, take a letter to the Secretary of State for Social Services, Alexander Fleming House, Elephant and Castle, SE1. Harold can take it across on the bus. I suppose everyone leaves there promptly at five o'clock, the Minister included. Dear Minister…' Faith flipped open her notebook. 'Say that in the name of ACHE, no British doctors must be allowed to leave the country from one minute after midnight. If our demand is not met instantly, we shan't call off the strike.'

' "…the strike in the Bertram Bunn Wing",' Faith supplied, writing in her book.

'No, the strike paralysing St Swithin's Hospital itself, from apex to boiler-house, from antenatal clinic to post-mortem room.'

'But we're not on strike in St Swithin's.'

'We are now.' He leapt on a bench. 'Brothers! Forward with the browncoats! Everybody out.'

# 15

'Brother browncoats! Fellow soldiers, in the van of mankind's ever-onward march against pestilence, privation and perishing.'

It was two hours later. Pip stood on a bench in the basement, his own brown coat flapping, arms upraised. Beside him on the concrete floor was Faith, holding her open notebook. He stared down at a hundred-odd faces, which stared back at him with a mass expression of mixed interest, scepticism and bafflement.

'During industrial peace, there's nothing so becomes a worker as modest stillness and humility,' Pip went on. 'But when the blast, "On strike!" blows in our ears, what do we do then?' He paused, as if waiting for a reply. 'I'll tell you. We imitate the action of the tiger. We stiffen the sinews, we summon up the blood. We disguise our normally fair nature with hard-favour'd rage. We lend our eye a terrible aspect.'

He stopped again, to judge the effect. The man in front's mouth had dropped open.

'Today, Brothers, I have taken a grave decision. You have all taken a grave decision. I made it on your behalf. And on behalf of the decent, working men and women, confined in their council houses up and down the country, who deserve a fair crack of the whip from the very section of the community expected to serve their most intimate needs. To wit, the doctors. I cannot say where our brave action will lead. Perhaps to the triumph of workers' natural virtues over capitalists' natural vice. I set no limits to my ambitions, which of course are also yours. Today St Swithin's, I say. Tomorrow the world! But I must ask you to be patient for an hour or two, while I explain exactly the issues which have incited you – through me – to choose this agonizingly serious option.'

The audience rose as a man and started filing through the door.

'Really, they could have been a bit more courteous,' Pip complained crossly to Faith, watching the last pair of brown-coated shoulders leave. 'After all, I *am* their democratically elected leader. They might possibly have found the rest of my speech a bit boring, but they could surely have sat through it with a fixed gaze thinking about football and sex and things, like I did often enough during your father's lectures in St Swithin's.'

'Poor Pip.' She stroked the back of his neck sympathetically, as they sat together on the hard bench. 'You put such desperately hard work into it since lunch.'

'I suppose some of that material about the differences in financing the current and capital programmes of the Health Service might have been a little beyond a few of them,' he admitted. 'But one can only try.' He looked up as Harold Sapworth strolled in, without his brown coat. 'My audience have walked out on me,' Pip complained.

'Go on?' Harold glanced at the wall clock. 'No wonder. It's just on three. Tea break.'

'But surely you can't take tea breaks when you're on strike anyway?' Pip said irritably.

'They still feel like a cuppa, I suppose. Besides, you sort of get in the habit. I goes on taking tea breaks when I'm lying on the beach on holiday.'

'Did you deliver the letter safely?' Faith asked.

'Easy. I got a forty-five bus. Funny, never been down the Elephant for years. Cousin of mine lives round there, in the New Kent Road. Or rather, he did. He shifted a year or two back to the Isle of Wight.'

'Did you hand it personally to the Minister?' Pip demanded severely.

'Well, not actual. Bloke with a flat hat and brass buttons downstairs said he'd take it up.'

'I suppose we have cast it into the usual channels, like bread upon the waters,' Pip reflected.

'And what do you suppose we shall find after several days?' Faith asked. 'Perhaps some extremely uneatable soggy slices?'

He looked at her. 'You're sounding a little doubtful.'

'I am. To be honest, I feel we've taken off a jumbo jet without knowing how to land it. You're not angry, are you, love?' she added quickly.

Pip said nothing for a moment, just nodding, elbows on knees, slowly rubbing his hands together.

'On the contrary, I feel rather like that, too. I think I could quite justly compare myself at the moment with Garibaldi, landing in Sicily at the head of his thousand red-shirted heroes. But he knew where to go. I don't. I can start a strike, that's obvious. Perhaps any fool can do that. But I've not the slightest idea how to run one. It's much more complicated than simply cutting off the delivery of minced chicken and bunches of flowers to the Bertie Bunn. All sorts of tricky problems must be sorted out. St Swithin's has obviously got to go on treating emergency cases – that seems traditional with hospital strikers, right across the world. So we've got to keep going the hot water, central sterile supply, fire precautions, and so on. Even the canteen. If they couldn't have their tea break, my members might not be one hundred per cent solidly enthusiastic.'

'Harold, you must have experienced a dozen strikes,' Faith suggested, as the porter was pulling on the first brown coat in sight.

'I've been through a few, that's straight. When I was sweeper in a car plant, we was called out so often I reckon some of the lads began to forget which end you put the engine in. They used to call us the Dagenham Kamikazes. That's a Jap car, ain't it?'

'What's the first principle in running a strike, then?' Pip asked him.

'Discipline,' Harold replied firmly, doing up the buttons. 'Keeping the lads in line. Arthur Pince was as useless at that as a bull's tit. Mind, Arthur was ginger.'

Pip frowned. 'I thought he was a small dark man?'

'Ginger beer. Queer,' Harold explained.

'I suppose discipline in the ranks depends on the use of my personality,' Pip decided thoughtfully.

'Use that if you like, mate. Personally, all the shop stewards what I know prefer a bit of the old –' He made his boxing motion. 'The reliable aggro.'

'I deplore the use of violence in any context.'

'Have it your own way,' Harold told him amiably. 'But if any of the lads gets less than wildly fanatic, then you've got to give them a bit of encouragement, by which I mean the flick knife in the car tyres, or maybe calling with a meat axe to do up their front room.'

'I think violence is perfectly justified,' Faith agreed with him. 'After all, in an army at war, any soldier who fails in his duty is shot on the spot.'

'Shooting's too good for some of them cowboys.' Harold nodded gloomily in the direction of the door. 'They want a bit of the old electricity where it tickles most.'

'Harold, I leave you in charge of morale,' Pip told him. 'Use whatever means you think best to maintain it, but stop short of murder.' He looked up in surprise as Forfar McBridie strode in, wearing Highland dress with bagpipes under his arm.

'I want to ask a straight question,' McBridie began. 'What's the strike got to offer Scotland?'

'I hadn't really given that aspect much thought,' replied Pip, annoyed at the intrusion.

'Well you'd better,' the Scotsman told him bluntly. 'I'm from Clydeside. That's where the real revolution's going to spring from. A great red river, rolling down the M6 to London. By the time we've finished, we'll make Culloden look like a pop festival.' He threw his head back, gazing starrily at the concrete ceiling. 'God save King Jamie the Eighth! Up from the Clydebank shipyards to Holyrood House. Scotland will be the richest nation in the world, because we control its two most precious fluids – oil and whisky.'

'As far as I'm concerned, there can be a King Clive in Cardiff and a King Arthur in Tintagel,' Pip told him shortly. 'And the Scots pound may be worth so much you can come down whenever you feel like it to buy up the Crown jewels, or spew diced carrots over Piccadilly, like after football matches – '

'I've a mind to slice your nose off,' declared Forfar McBridie angrily, reaching for his skean-dhu.

'Harold, administer the disciplinary treatment,' Pip ordered. 'Listen, Mr McBridie. This strike is on behalf of decent men and women throughout the country, not just bits of it. Who are *you*?' he demanded abruptly of a thin, wispy lady who had just ventured through the door, wearing a long fringed dress and a yellowish straw hat which appeared to have been mislaid for some time under other heavy articles.

'Mr Cripps, is it?' she asked throatily. 'They said I should find you here. I saw you in the papers. What are you going to do about the doggies?'

Pip scratched his stiff fair hair. 'Doggies are nothing to do with us. This strike is directed against doctors, not vets.'

'Oh, but they *are* to do with you,' the lady continued earnestly. 'You're the man, Mr Cripps, who can do something about our poor doggies. You must stop them smoking.'

'You are referring, I suppose,' said Faith, 'to dogs in experiments, given tobacco smoke to find the cause of cancer?'

'Exactly, Miss. It's wicked. Unspeakably wicked. The poor doggies. It's bad enough, people who encourage children to smoke. But doggies!'

'I suppose it hasn't occurred to you,' Faith continued coolly, 'that the experiments will probably save thousands of human lives?'

'I'm not interested in that. It's cruel to the doggies. It's not that they even like smoking. Whoever saw a doggie smoke of its own free will? You must put a stop to it, Mr Cripps,' she instructed Pip firmly. 'Don't call off your strike until every doggie in the country has been released by these mad scientists to breathe God's fresh air. And baboons –'

'Stop!' Pip jumped up, hands over ears. 'I am running, with extreme difficulty, a strike at St Swithin's for one specific purpose. And everyone seems intent on climbing on the bandwagon for their own selfish reasons. Yet if I lose sight of my purpose – which is simply to stop doctors ratting on their fellow countrymen – I'm lost. That's exactly how Julius Caesar came to grief. And Napoleon. Trying to fight too many people at once. Harold, deal with this lady. Perhaps you could organize some sort of industrial action at the Battersea Dogs' Home?'

Harold Sapworth sucked the tip of his thumb. 'Funny, but I was just going to ask you a favour, too. That cousin what I just mentioned, down in the New Kent Road. It's not that he wanted to go to the Isle of Wight, actual. He's doing a bit of bird there. Eight years, with good behaviour. Mind, he was innocent. I know the bloke it was, what carved up the postmistress. But if you could keep up the strike until justice was done –'

'No, no, no!' Pip smacked a fist into his palm. 'I've half a mind to call it off, here and now. A strike is a matter of standing up for your principles, not of blackmail.'

'Can't see much difference, myself. They has to buy you off in either case. It's just a matter of fixing the right price. Still, don't put yourself out. I never cared much for my cousin, anyway. Besides, his old woman's enjoying having it off with all and sundry. I collected these letters for you upstairs,' he added, thrusting a pair of envelopes into Pip's hand.

Pip strode to the far corner of the basement, sat down alone, and opened the first envelope. It said,

*Dear Chipps,*

*I understand from your aunt that you have taken employment as a hospital porter, and are interesting yourself in industrial relations. I congratulate you. It is a subject sadly thin in the attention of first-class academic minds, such as I believe you to possess. You may not feel this compliment either sincere or acceptable after the exchanges of our last meeting. But I assure you that I have always considered you academically sound, if utterly disastrous in practice. Will you kindly be on my ward round at Virtue by ten o'clock tomorrow morning. You will learn something to your eventual advantage.*

*Yours,*

*Lancelot Spratt.*

'I wonder what that crafty old hyena's up to?' Pip muttered. 'I suppose I'd better go along. At least, he daren't make me look a fool any more in front of everybody, including the patient.'

The second envelope contained a telephone message. He read it, jumped up with a shout, and sprang across to Faith and Harold Sapworth, who were arguing with the intruders in the doorway. 'It's all right,' Pip exclaimed. 'We can go ahead with absolute confidence. We've been taken seriously. Look at this – it's from the BBC. They want me to appear on television.' He tugged down the lapels of his brown coat. 'Tonight,' he said breathlessly, 'I address the nation.'

# 16

'Good evening. This Thursday we have with us in the studio the man who has turned himself into a national figure overnight. A feat which is usually reserved for footballers and pop singers. And of course kidnapped children. Yesterday, ACHE – the health employees' union – went on strike against the private patients of St Swithin's Hospital in London. This afternoon, the whole of this world-famous hospital containing more than one thousand beds was brought to a standstill. What caused you to take this drastic action, Mr Chipps?'

'Well, Robin, it was simply to force the Government to implement our ban on doctors emigrating.'

'But that's nothing to do with the running of the hospital, surely? I mean, the daily portering and cleaning and laundering and so on, which members of ACHE are concerned in?'

'Oh, nothing to do with it whatever. The strike weapon is the only means we trade unions have of getting our demands promptly and fully met. It is our only weapon for obtaining social justice. Which of course is the same thing.'

'Come, now, Mr Chipps. You mean that yours is a political strike?'

'All strikes are political these days, Robin. Now that the Government is so tightly enmeshed in absolutely every national enterprise, whether State-run, commercial or supposedly independent.'

'But isn't it hard on the patients, Mr Chipps? Or even dangerous? I mean, I shouldn't like to be taken to St Swithin's with some acute and painful illness, and be turned away at the front door.'

'You wouldn't, Robin. All emergency cases are being treated as usual.'

The interviewer twitched his bow tie and assumed the expression of amiable inquiry at which Cabinet Ministers had been known to blanch and wonder what exactly he had dug up from their best-forgotten past speeches. 'And who decides which is an emergency and which isn't?'

'ACHE do, Robin.'

'Don't the doctors at St Swithin's object to ACHE taking over their functions?'

'The doctors in a modern hospital are not in a position to object about anything. They are just beginning to find that out.'

'Do you honestly think that you yourself are in a position, Mr Chipps, to dictate to the medical profession? With traditions somewhat stronger and a history a good deal longer than those of ACHE?'

'I honestly think that I am, Robin.'

'Thank you, Mr Chipps.'

'Thank you, Robin.'

'Turn off that rubbish instantly,' ordered the matron of the Bertram Bunn Wing, who had come into Brenda Bristols' room shortly after seven o'clock bearing a plate of sandwiches. 'You might be interested to know that I have cut almost one thousand sandwiches for the patients' suppers with my own hands.'

'Lovely,' said Brenda Bristols, sitting up in bed in her transparent nightie. 'I'm ravenous. What sort are they?'

'Ham and pickled onions. The time for anything fancy is past. *What* are you still doing in this patient's room?' she demanded of Lord Hopcroft, who was sitting in the armchair in his short nightshirt.

'I was getting some advice from Miss Bristols on my condition. Your computer downstairs really comes into its own with this present trying situation. It functions as efficiently as ever, strike or no strike. The latest print-out says I'm suffering from pre-eclampsia.'

'That's impossible,' she told him shortly. 'It's a disease of pregnancy.'

'But I explained when you found me in the bathroom, Matron, that I *am* pregnant. And according to the computer this afternoon, I'm almost in labour. It's certainly a quick worker.'

'Lord Hopcroft, I should have imagined that *you* enjoyed a sense of humour more remote from that of our medical students.'

'But I'm not joking,' he complained. 'I'm simply pointing out how the computer has made a mistake.'

'The computer does not make mistakes. That is impossible.'

'Couldn't do us a bottle of bubbly too, dear?' asked Brenda Bristols, doubtfully inspecting the interior of a sandwich. 'I need a bit of cheering up.'

'I could not. This strike obliges us all to make sacrifices. You will have to go for once without champagne. I am already late for a vital meeting with Sir Lancelot Spratt in my office.'

'Do give the lovely man a great big kiss from me.'

'I shall do nothing of the kind,' the matron told her icily. 'Sir Lancelot and myself share a professional relationship with no object but the welfare of our patients.'

'What about ham sandwiches for me?' inquired Lord Hopcroft.

'Meat is forbidden in pre-eclampsia,' she told him, sweeping out.

Once through the door, the matron glanced at the watch dangling at her left breast. Sir Lancelot would already be there. But she had an important diversion on her way down to the office. She dodged through the nearest door marked 'Ladies'. Staring into the washbasin mirror, she produced from her uniform pocket a box of make-up and carefully applied it round her eyes. Such brazenness was really unthinkable in uniform. But that night she was to spring her most powerful assault, and everyone said that her eyes were her best feature. She could not allow Sir Lancelot to float about loose with such ravenous predators as Brenda Bristols lying in wait to snap him up. She replaced the make-up box and took out a little gold spray, applying a short burst of scent behind either ear. The girl in the boutique had assured her that it was as irresistible as chopped liver to a hungry mastiff.

She opened the door of her steel and glass cubicle by the front entrance to find Sir Lancelot perched on her desk with feet dangling, glancing idly through his half-moon glasses at an open evening paper.

'Good evening, Lancelot.'

'Evening.'

She stood smoothing the front of her blue dress. He went on reading the paper.

113

'Lancelot, this is the end of civilization as we knew it,' she decided to open the conversation.

'I am aware of trouble in t'ward,' he returned calmly. 'But I fancy it will soon evaporate in its own hot air.'

'This nephew of mine has developed megalomania. Just like Stalin and his doctors' plot. Did you see Pip on television?'

'I only watch the cricket.' Sir Lancelot still did not look up.

'The way these greedy unions grab everything they can these days is utterly terrifying. I honestly don't know why the workers are always out after more money. What can they find to spend it on? They get free medicine and free education, subsidized food, housing and transport, free pensions in their old age. They do nothing but dissipate their wages on package tours and bingo. There ought to be a law against it.'

'Oh, laws won't do anything,' he observed. 'Parliament doesn't signify, now the country's run in this peculiar way by the Trades Union Congress, with public opinion forming Her Majesty's Opposition.' Sir Lancelot looked up at last, sniffing. 'Somebody been using ether, Matron? I thought the anaesthetists had given up that smelly stuff years ago. The unions will obviously get away with all they can, like every other individual or organization or nation in history.' He turned his eyes down to his paper. 'Anyway, democratic trade unions are self-defeating organisms. First they bankrupt their employers then they establish Communism. Fortunately, the process takes time and even the British people wake up sooner or later. Or at least stir in their sleep.'

'So you don't think anything can be done to settle this atrocious strike?' she asked in a depressed voice.

'On the contrary, I intend to settle it myself tomorrow morning.'

She looked at him in disbelief, which was swiftly chased off her features by adoration. 'Oh, Lancelot,' she exclaimed. 'But how?'

'On my ward round.' He folded the newspaper and put it on the desk. 'Which I have specifically requested your young man to attend. He is simply exhibiting in virulent form the syndrome I continually observe in my newly qualified students. A sudden rush of importance to the head can produce the most alarming signs and symptoms. He is moreover suffering from an overdose of bigotry, which is the most heady of drugs. Fortunately, a cure is simple. A fierce enough jab in the vitals, and the self-inflation collapses with a loud pop.'

'Oh, Lancelot,' she repeated. 'Every day in every way, I admire you more and more.'

'What's Pip's father think of all this, by the way?'

'I haven't heard a word. But he probably approves. He's a man of violently eccentric ideas himself.'

'The only idea of Pip's father which I can remember was retiring to a tiny practice in Somerset and doing as little work as possible for as little money as possible to live on. Hardly anything eccentric in that.'

'Oh, Lancelot.' She came close to the desk. 'I knew from the start of this dreadful business that it called for a man of your calibre to control events. The dean simply dithers.'

'I agree. When the medical profession is faced with a situation which confronts the owners of steam laundries or sausage factories every week, they run about like hens in a cloudburst. Are you somewhat dehydrated?' he broke off.

'I – I don't think so,' she replied, puzzled.

'You've rather nasty dark rings under your eyes, that's all. We medical people did live in such a cosy world before the hospital unions realized their own strength,' he resumed. 'As one politician put it, there was a gulf in outlook, sympathy and comprehension between the tight little, warm little inside world of a hospital and the peculiar, unreasonable, ungrateful creatures we observed outside through the windows.'

'Which politician?'

'Mr Enoch Powell.'

'Oh, him,' she said dismissively.

'He was one of our few Ministers of Health who did not regard the job primarily as a stepping stone to a better one.'

'Oh, Lancelot – ' She drew closer. 'You're so erudite.'

'As I explained, it's simply that since I became a widower I am able to do a great deal of reading in bed.'

She dropped her voice, the crested bosom of her dress against his arm. 'But isn't reading in bed a desperately lonely pastime?'

'One can hardly be lonely with the great Victorian novelists, and their vividly drawn galleries of entertaining characters.'

'Of course, you're so right...' Her thigh pressed his. 'I read novels, too, when I'm not over-exhausted from my day's work. Perhaps we...you and I...could both go to sleep with your favourite author?'

'Trollope.'

'How dare you,' she screeched, slapping him so hard she knocked off his glasses.

'He was a contemporary of Dickens,' Sir Lancelot told her wearily, picking them up. 'How's Miss Bristols? I'll operate on her tomorrow afternoon, if I can get this strike over. I feel inclined to add a substantial sum to my fee for the free publicity.'

He left the matron standing open-mouthed, pinker than ever.

'A good try,' he decided to himself, stepping across the deserted entrance hall. 'Eye-shadow, perfume, the lot. The poor dear must be getting desperate. Thank Heavens I've this peculiar Bristols female to hide behind.' He stopped, surprised to find himself confronted by Mr Grout. Sir Lancelot had never known anyone from the administrator's office to be in the hospital after five o'clock, even to visit their own sick relatives. He noticed with interest the junior administrator was accompanied by a slim young woman in a short smart dress and blonde hair arranged in a style he supposed could be named a tonsorial turban.

'This,' Mr Grout explained to her, as though indicating some famed national monument, 'is the surgeon, Sir Lancelot Spratt.'

'Delighted to meet you, Sir Lancelot,' she said with a slight accent, offering a slim-fingered hand.

'Dr Langenbeck is from Hamburg, a doctor of philosophy,' Mr Grout explained with a look of self-satisfaction which would have befitted his senior. 'She is studying conditions in British hospitals.'

'Charmed, madam.' Sir Lancelot bowed slightly. 'Have you visited London before?'

'No, but my father has, often.'

'Where does he stay?'

'He didn't. He was in the Luftwaffe.'

'You must find Old England quite ridiculously degenerate,' Sir Lancelot said amiably.

'Quite the opposite. You are highly efficient. Your strikes are superbly organized and executed. No German worker could get within a kilometre of such successful operations.'

Sir Lancelot inclined himself again. 'I always accept compliments avidly, particularly when they are well deserved.'

'I should much like to meet your Mr Chipps. He seems a very intelligent and vigorous young man. In Germany, they would invite him at once to join the board of directors, whether of a manufacturing firm or of a hospital like St Swithin's.'

'Unfortunately, in this country the workers and bosses see themselves as two sides in a game of cup-tie football. They combine together only for international contests, which thank God seem to be a thing of the past. If you can be at my ward tomorrow by ten, I'll see if I can effect an introduction to Mr Chipps. I take it you are in London overnight?'

'Yes, Charlie is taking me out to dinner.' Sir Lancelot was for a moment mystified. 'But not again, please, to that awful canteen,' she smiled at Mr Grout. 'Fried fish and peas. Ugh. And that pink sauce like hot floor-polish.'

'Could you recommend a decent restaurant, Sir Lancelot?' Mr Grout asked eagerly. 'I'm not footing the...I mean, it's official entertainment.'

'They tell me that the Mirabelle in Curzon Street is very tolerable. I hope you have an instructive visit to our country, Dr Langenbeck.'

'I'm sure I shall. I have spent much time in preparation, you know. I have read all your great writers who have analysed British politics and the British nation.'

Sir Lancelot nodded slowly. 'My dear Doctor, there are only two of our commentators who accurately understood the British people, their institutions and their politics. As you can tell from encountering their work any day.'

The blonde frowned. 'Who? Gibbon and Macaulay?'

'No. Gilbert and Sullivan. Good night.'

# 17

Precisely at ten that Friday morning, and precisely as usual, Sir Lancelot Spratt strode through the plate-glass doors into Virtue surgical ward of St Swithin's Hospital.

The ward itself had changed vastly since his first entry to the old Virtue Ward in the now demolished building as its consultant surgeon. In those orderly days, it contained two straight well-disciplined lines of patients, drilled by the ward sister, it seemed to Sir Lancelot, to breathe in unison. The rebuilt hospital was all nooks and crannies, patients in twos and threes all over the place. Even men mixed up with women, which would have made the old ward sisters stare and even resign. But Sir Lancelot supposed the mingling was a convenience to his surgical colleague upstairs, who specialized in sex-change operations, and where you could never tell if his wards were male, female or undecided.

But in any modern hospital ward, Sir Lancelot reflected as he marched along, the surroundings made little difference. The patients spent their time staring at television, except the ones who were unconscious. The surgeon progressed with something of his old retinue, like an Emperor fallen on seedy times who must cut down the ceremonial. He was followed by his white-coated assistants, his white-jacketed students and his ward sister, whom he vaguely understood to have become under the modern administration something like Principal Nursing Officer Grade Seven (Female) Permanent and Pensionable.

Sir Lancelot crossed briskly to a bed in the far corner, containing a pinched-looking youngish man staring about him nervously. A few yards from the foot stood the German doctor of philosophy. By the patient's head was Pip in his brown coat, beside him Faith.

'Good morning, Mr Chipps,' the surgeon began.

'Good morning, Sir Lancelot.'

'Good morning, Faith. You're looking blooming. Getting plenty of tennis?'

'Good morning, Uncle Lancelot.'

Sir Lancelot briefly introduced Dr Langenbeck, then rubbed his hands as though about to start a good breakfast. 'Well, Mr Chipps. I'm pleased to see you on my round this morning. Perhaps you'd kindly give me your opinion of this case?'

'Diagnosis first?' Pip asked.

'If you wish.'

'It's not an emergency.'

Sir Lancelot nodded his head several times sagely. 'Well, Mr Chipps. You have taken a full case history, and performed your physical examination?'

'Yes, Sir Lancelot. And it's definitely not an emergency.'

'We'll go over the symptoms,' the surgeon continued helpfully. 'Umbilical pain starting at two in the morning, vomiting and diarrhoea.' Pip nodded agreement. 'Anything else?'

Pip stood scratching his wiry hair. Sir Lancelot reminded him, 'And fever.'

'Am I going to be all right, Doctor?' asked the patient anxiously.

'Now don't you pay any attention to our medical talk, my dear fellow,' Sir Lancelot reassured him. 'It happens to be necessary for your own good that I should discuss your case with this other doctor here. Our words may sound rather alarming, but they're only technical terms, "shop talk".'

'He looks more like a porter to me,' the patient grumbled.

'We have run out of white coats,' Sir Lancelot explained, 'because of industrial trouble in the hospital laundry. I may have to operate stark naked under my gown, but we're here with the one object of getting you better as quickly as possible. So just lie back in your comfortable bed and relax. That's the way to help us. Now, Mr Chipps. On examination?'

'Pain and tenderness in the umbilical region extending to the right iliac fossa.'

'When can I have something to drink, Doctor?' came from the pillow.

'All in good time. Please don't interrupt. We are having a serious discussion. And rigidity, Mr Chipps?'

'Yes, Sir Lancelot. In the right iliac fossa.'

'I could do with a bottle of beer, and no mistake.'

'Once you're on the mend, you can consume a barrel, if you feel like it. So you stick to your diagnosis?' Sir Lancelot raised his thick eyebrows.

'Yes. Not an emergency.'

'Come now,' he invited amiably. 'Think again. My dear Mr Chipps, even in your first week here as a surgical dresser, you could hardly have missed a barn-door diagnosis like this. Umbilical pain, vomiting, fever, right-sided tenderness and rigidity – that can't add up to anything but acute appendicitis, surely?'

'What about the diarrhoea?' Pip asked with a crafty look. 'That doesn't fit in.'

'You get diarrhoea frequently in appendicitis,' Sir Lancelot told him abrasively. 'Listen, you stupid berk – I mean, my dear sir. If you don't believe me, you can go down to the hospital library and look it all up in Bailey and Love's textbook of surgery.'

'*I* think it's bacillary dysentery.'

'Balderdash.'

'Well, it's my opinion that counts,' Pip pointed out to the surgeon politely.

'It's an appendix, you bloody fool,' roared Sir Lancelot.

Pip drew his brown coat round him. 'That's hardly the way to address a colleague. Very unprofessional language. Might I ask you to observe normal etiquette?'

Sir Lancelot's beard appeared to bristle. 'If this patient isn't operated upon within the hour, he'll die.'

The patient gave a shriek. 'Don't take any notice of our doctors' talk,' Sir Lancelot instructed him hastily. He turned to Pip. 'So stop obstructing the work of this hospital with your arrogant and obstinate ignorance.'

'I don't want to die,' whimpered the patient, pulling bedclothes to chin.

'Please, what in German is "balderdash"?' interrupted Dr Langenbeck mildly.

'*Dummes Zeug*,' Sir Lancelot threw in her direction.

'*Me* arrogant,' returned Pip hotly. 'For years, Sir Lancelot, you've been parading round this hospital as a complete autocrat. Without one word of kindness, of acknowledgement, even of recognition to your fellow toilers in the wards with mop and bucket or a tea trolley.'

'If he does die, he'll be on your ruddy conscience to the end of your days, not mine.' Sir Lancelot jabbed a finger towards the patient, who gave another shriek and started climbing out of bed. 'Just relax, my good fellow, relax,' Sir Lancelot advised him. 'If you don't, you may burst something nasty inside.'

'Conscience! You talk to me about conscience. What conscience have you got about the staff of this hospital, who are exploited on poverty wages for all the heavy shifting and swabbing?'

'Listen, you maladjusted Tolpuddle Martyr,' barked Sir Lancelot, not noticing that the patient was now lying under the bed. 'I came along this morning perfectly confident that I could get your little nonsense called off by showing you up in public as a bloody fool. I failed. Simply because you reveal yourself as a more ruthless, desperate and inhuman little upstart than I imagined. But I happen to put my patients first, even before my principles. I am therefore now trying to talk to you sensibly, as a fellow member of the medical profession, as a former student of St Swithin's who might well become one again – '

'What's that? Again?' Pip interrupted eagerly. 'I could be reinstated?'

'Of course you could. That is a solution to everybody's difficulties which I am at a loss to understand was conceived by nobody. I shall have a word with the dean this morning. The medical school may be outside my province, but the need for action is desperate and when it comes to twisting the dean's arm he is compliantly double-jointed. Where's the patient?'

The man was crawling on his elbows, trying to get through the ring of feet round the bed.

'That's a genuine, sincere offer?' asked Pip.

'I never make offers which are otherwise. Providing you allow me to operate on this patient, of course.'

Pip grinned. 'I was going to, anyway. I was just enjoying putting you in your place. I've been longing to do precisely as much for years. So has everyone in St Swithin's, if it comes to that.'

Sir Lancelot glared for some moments. 'Pick this patient up from the floor and get him down to the theatre at once. Tell anaesthetics that he has had no pre-medication,' he instructed his assistants, repeating the orders in Hindi. 'Don't go away, Chipps,' he added, as Pip began sidling from the bedside. 'Nor you, Faith. I have something special to say. You see that lady with the fair hair? She is from Germany.'

'I am studying your National Health Service,' Dr Langenbeck explained to Pip. 'Which your politicians repeatedly indicate as the envy of all civilized nations.'

'She is also preserving perfect decorum,' Sir Lancelot went on, 'while doubtless squirming with laughter inside, at the spectacle of the idiot way in which this country of ours – well within my memory, ruler of the greatest Empire the modern world has known – is tearing itself to bits less through selfishness, envy and laziness than through a degree of bloody-mindedness which makes Dracula look like a milksop. You should be ashamed of yourself, Chipps. You don't seem to have one patriotic chromosome in your entire set of genes.'

Pip answered evenly, 'Patriotism is only the capitalists' way of getting the workers to die for them suddenly instead of slowly.'

'I shall ignore that remark. If I did not, I should beat you over the head with the bedpan that nurse is carrying past.'

'Please, what is a milksop?' inquired Dr Langenbeck.

'*Schwächling.*'

'I find your English jokes sometimes very difficult to follow.'

'As for Faith, Chipps, you are not fit to share the same street with her, let alone the same shack. What is it?' Sir Lancelot demanded testily as the browncoated Harold Sapworth pushed past his elbow.

'Pip, there's hundreds of blokes from the newspapers outside,' Harold told him excitedly. 'Telly vans, radio, the lot. Since you was on the box last night, almost every hospital in the country's come out in sympathy. They wants you to hold a press conference.'

Pip drew himself up. 'I have stopped the entire National Health Service,' he said breathlessly. 'Well! Fancy that.' He stared wide-eyed, seeing neither Sir Lancelot nor anyone. 'Power.' He opened and closed his fists. 'The power of television, which is real life to the oppressed poor who struggle with their sordid ones…' He continued whispering to himself, 'I, Pip Chipps, addressed them sitting in their own homes… Power, lovely power…' He jerked back to reality, adding decisively to Faith, 'Right. I shall hold a press conference forthwith.' He raised his clenched fist. 'Workers of the NHS unite! Remember the Three Day Week War. This is yet another but more famous victory.'

Pip strode from the ward, Faith and Harold Sapworth at his heels. A second later, he imagined he was being assassinated.

As Pip had stepped into the corridor, a man hurled himself forward knocking him into the arms of his followers. After a second, Pip judged the assailant to be simply another of his admirers, from the manner in which he was grovelling, embracing Pip's ankles and his unpolished zipped boots. His adulator appeared a wizened, dusky fellow, wearing a towelling dressing-gown issued by St Swithin's to patients who for reasons of poverty or emergency arrived ill-equipped.

'Master, master,' cried the man at Pip's feet. 'Save me, save me.'

'Something the matter?' he asked.

'Master, I know you. Everyone in my ward knows you. Mr Chipps, the most powerful personage in St Swithin's.'

'If not the whole country,' Pip corrected him in a modest voice.

'You have the power of life and death. My life and death. Please, sir, I implore you.' His face gazed up tear-stained from the floor. 'Cardiac transplantation. The operation is not by any manner of means an emergency, is it?'

Pip scratched his chin. 'Might be difficult to say.'

'Please, Master, decide that it is not an emergency. Then it cannot be done. At least, it cannot be done this morning. Oh, Master! I am a poor man. But I will sell all my goods in Shanka and make you a lovely present if only you will decide that I am not an emergency. You can take my beautiful daughter as a household slave, what you in England call an *au pair*.'

'It's a really difficult diagnosis,' Pip announced ponderingly. 'What do you say, Harold? Is a heart transplant an emergency operation or isn't it?'

'Real dodgy, that one,' Harold Sapworth agreed. 'Could be, or couldn't. Reckon you'd have to refer it to the executive of ACHE. Maybe even the President. It's one of them fundamental decisions, like the demarcation rules in the Scottish shipyards.'

'Exactly.' Pip nodded. 'I should like to call in a second opinion,' he told the grovelling patient. 'You'll probably hear within a week or two.'

'But I must know this minute,' he objected agonizedly. 'My surgeon is all ready to operate, he is sterilizing his special knife, the biggest knife I have seen in all my born days, oh my goodness.'

'And who is your surgeon?'

'Professor Ding,' he replied with quivering cheeks.

'Oh, yes. The one we call the Black Barnard.'

'He is the black something else, let me tell you,' the patient said grimly. 'Moreover, he is my brother-in-law. There is nothing wrong with me, I am as healthy as any astronaut.' He thumped his chest. 'But my brother-in-law, he wants to make a meal of my heart, just to get the Order of the White Rhino and a blooming great backhander.'

He started shaking all over as a roar came from the end of the corridor. In green gown and cap, rubber gloves on hands, mask dangling below unsmiling face, Professor Ding came charging upon his patient.

'What's the bleeding idea, you escaping from the anaesthetic room, just as I am all tooled up and ready for work?' he demanded furiously. 'Walk out on us, hey? With me and my assistants, anaesthetists, nurses, fifty people, all putting themselves out on account of saving your health and life. Some people ain't got no gratitude,' he complained, eyes rolling in the direction of Pip. 'On your feet, Sonny Boy. You and me going back to the operating theatre in double-quick time, carry on the good work, and you're gonna lie back and enjoy it, get me?'

The patient was on his knees, hands clasped in prayer directed at Pip. Professor Ding seized the nape of his scrawny neck and jerked him erect. 'I say,' frowned Pip. 'What is all this, exactly?'

Professor Ding found his usual broad grin. 'This patient a bit nervous. He spending all week, just waiting for his operation, playing Scrabble, bloody stupid game. Enough to get the old nerves frayed in anyone. This morning comes his big chance. Some stupid bugger gets run over right on St Swithin's doorstep, by one of them TV vans driving through the gate. Casualty reckon they gotta stiff on their hands. But, "Oh no," I says. "Ha ha," I says. "The old ticker in the corpse beat away lub-dup, lub-dup down the old stethoscope, exactly as described in the famous textbook, *The Student's Companion*". I tells them to connect him up to the mains, keep the old breathing going, though bits of him are as dead as a load of doornails. Boy! I says to myself. We're gonna start the big production number here and now. I goes up to the ward to tell this ungrateful sod – ' He gave his patient a violent shake. 'Just to put new heart in him – '

Professor Ding paused. His grin widened, his natural good humour bubbled through his professional disapprobation. 'I put new heart in him! You get it? I make a joke.'

'You told the theatre porters it was an emergency operation?' Pip asked.

'Sure. Our glorious President and Field Marshal and Minister of Health in Shanka, he reckon a heart swap an emergency. Gotta be done quick, to put Shanka on the map afore the next International Health Congress start dishing out the funds for cardiac research and all that jazz. Mind, we don't have all that much cardiac research going on just this moment in Shanka,' admitted the professor. 'But the lolly come in mighty useful for other expenses.'

'What's your opinion, Faith?'

'Look, Mister – the corpse is red-hot, just right,' Professor Ding told Pip urgently. 'But what happen after he bin connected to the old respirator a few hours, maybe days? He go off, like bad fish. Heart no good for nothing but cat meat. I gotta slice this carcass right now. Besides, think of all the electric juice what the stiff is consuming at the hospital's expense.'

'To my mind,' Faith said precisely, 'the emergency concerns the cardiac donor. The recipient you are holding by the back of the neck, Professor Ding, looks in no need of immediate treatment. In fact, he seems to be struggling away very healthily. But as the donor in the respirator is already dead, how can he present the need for a life-saving operation? So it isn't an emergency, QED.'

Giving a yell, the patient broke from the Professor's grasp and disappeared with trailing dressing-gown round the corner.

'Come back, you ungrateful little bleeder,' shouted Professor Ding furiously, giving chase. 'You just wait till I got my knife into you, I'm gonna cut off a few bits what'll spoil your Saturday nights, you just wait and see. And don't forget that hundred bucks what you borrowed, *and* it's about time you let me have back my automatically winding self-focusing reflex, which I reckon you gone and flogged at the second-hand shop…'

The noise died away. 'Come,' said Pip firmly. 'It is only ethical that we should turn aside for our professional duties, despite keeping so many busy people waiting downstairs.' He buttoned up his brown coat and threw back his shoulders. 'I shall now meet the Press.'

# 18

'No,' said the dean. 'Definitely, unequivocally and inflexibly no.'

'But my dear Dean! Surely you must see how so simple an action would instantly end this distressing and uncomfortable episode in the hospital's history?' countered Sir Lancelot.

'I would no sooner reinstate Chipps in the medical school than invite a Soho vice king round to tea with my family.'

'But his reinstatement would be hailed as a move of diplomatic brilliance,' Sir Lancelot urged. The contentious appendix had been removed, and they were standing in the main hall of St Swithin's during the middle of that afternoon. Sir Lancelot noticed that despite the strike it seemed to contain as many lost visitors as ever. 'Something worthy of a Disraeli or a Talleyrand or that fat fellow who keeps getting on and off aeroplanes.'

'No,' said the dean.

'You don't seem to give any thought to the patients,' Sir Lancelot told him gruffly.

'I have put my patients first all my life. Despite personal considerations which were at times overwhelming. Now they are irresistibly so.'

'If you're so stiff-necked and pig-headed that you can't climb down for once,' Sir Lancelot said crossly, 'then you must have a smaller mind than even I imagined, all these years I have been obliged to listen to its jejune outpourings.'

'Insults will get you nowhere, Lancelot,' the dean responded primly. 'Though in fact you might have taken the words from my mouth about yourself. It is not that I refuse to admit 1 was wrong. No medical man would ever refuse that.'

'No, if only because the necessity seems to happen so often.'

'But I will not countenance in the medical school the man who…who shacked up my daughter.'

'We can't go about bleating like our professional moralists,' Sir Lancelot said in exasperation. 'We've got to accept human beings as they are. That's the first thing you learn in medicine, surely? Young persons have been doing what you describe with considerable vigour for centuries. It is merely that they are more open about it than in the days of Little Nell, or Nell Gwynn for that matter. Anyway, an awful lot of it's boasting. People these days seem to enjoy a remarkable conceit about their abilities at sex or driving.'

'She is not your daughter,' the dean said in a vinegary voice. 'She is mine. Besides, the young man has always struck me as looking highly insanitary.'

'That's your last word?'

'Indubitably.'

'So the strike will go on,' Sir Lancelot observed gloomily. 'Perhaps for years. Some do, even when the pickets have completely forgotten what it was all about.'

'I am past caring. Civilization is over. Chaos reigns. The Creator has announced *Fiat nox* and switched off. I'm going for my tea.' The dean slipped into a lift just as the doors closed.

Sir Lancelot gave a heavy sigh. The dean was an obstinate fool, and the opinions of obstinate fools were more trouble to eradicate than greenfly in roses. He took another lift down to the sub-basement car park. He knew that he could blackmail the dean with threats of spiking his pet projects on hospital committees, or revealing his behaviour after the last rugger club dinner. But that took time, and settling the strike was urgent. He crossed thoughtfully to the Rolls in his reserved parking space. He disliked putting to use his influential patients, but the simple coincidence of his professional visit that afternoon was too tempting to be overlooked.

Sir Lancelot drove up the winding concrete slope, stacked on either side with plastic bags of smelly rubbish, the local refuse collectors having 'blacked' it. Strange, those emotional words, he ruminated. 'Black' or 'red' or 'strike' itself stirred deep emotions in rugged breasts. So did 'lock-out' or 'victimization' or 'boss', or in a different sense 'workers'. He could have agreed with Pip that politics was really simple practical psychology. And industrial disputes were founded not upon money, which could only buy things, but upon power, which was pride. Meanwhile, he reflected as he drove westwards, it was useful to play the worm in so many powerful men's confidences.

Sir Lancelot drew up his Rolls at the kerb. A policeman saluted. Nodding acknowledgement, clutching his square black leather instrument case, he made for the front door. A lurking young man immediately stepped forward with, 'Excuse me – but you would be Sir Lancelot Spratt the surgeon, I believe?'

'Well, I don't look like the Leader of the Opposition, do I?' he returned testily.

'Is there any particular significance in your visit?' his interceptor asked eagerly. 'I represent the *Daily*—'

'My dear young man, mine is purely a routine call which is never reported in the Press. The appearance of medical persons on the doorsteps of great men can have effects which are widespread and often devastating. Currencies crumble, stock exchanges collapse, armies march. I have an arrangement to prevent such catastrophes occurring regularly once a month. You should have checked with your editor.'

The front door had already opened, in the hands of a tail-coated butler. Inside was a lean, youngish Civil Servant, dressed with the same formality of the surgeon.

'Good afternoon, Sir Lancelot.' The surgeon had got to know the official well over the past few years. 'I'm afraid Mr Nelson is still in committee. He'll be with you as soon as possible.'

Sir Lancelot nodded. 'I assume he's been keeping well?'

'As fit as a flea. Or should I say some other insect?' The Civil Servant smiled, being one of the few in the secret. 'Mrs Nelson is in the garden tatting. She wondered if you'd care to join her for a cup of tea and a cigarette?'

'I don't smoke, and I would not intrude upon a lady's afternoon's peace. I'll go straight upstairs.'

Sir Lancelot stepped into the narrow automatic lift. Mr and Mrs

Herbert Nelson lived in a cramped flat above the official rooms which filled most of the old, oft-renovated building. In the bedroom, Sir Lancelot removed his jacket, rolled up the sleeves of his white shirt, and opened the leather case on a chair. His eye travelled round the now familiar personal items in the room – the group photograph of Mr Nelson in his youthful football team, his framed life-saving certificate and coloured commendation from Sunday school, two texts in pokerwork *Wine Maketh Merry: But Money Answereth All Things Ecclesiastes X* 19 and *There Are More Ways to Kill A Cat Than Choking It With Cream*. He noticed again the small shelf of well-thumbed books, *Lamb's Tales From Shakespeare*, *The Golden Treasury*, *The Plain Man's Guide to Wine*, *Teach Yourself Economics*. He genuinely was the simple man he liked to see depicted in the newspapers, Sir Lancelot decided indulgently. The surgeon was inspecting a small ceramic article of baffling use inscribed *Clovelly*, with a year indicating purchase on the Nelsons' honeymoon, when the bedroom door opened and his patient hurried in.

'Afternoon, Sir Lancelot. I was at a very long and very tough confrontation with the people from the Autoworkers Union. About the National Bubble.'

'The little plastic car which threatened to make our streets resemble rivers floating with ping-pong balls?'

'That's the snag. No one wants to buy it. We're thinking of giving 'em away – first to deserving persons, old age pensioners, unmarried mothers and that. Then to anyone prepared to drive 'em off. Trouble is, the Autoworkers' executive aren't content with our ban on the import of foreign cars. They want Parliament to pass a law making all foreigners buy British ones. I explained that quite frankly for technical reasons it wouldn't work.' He started taking down his trousers. 'How do these political slogans appeal to you, Sir Lancelot? *Inflation Means More Money. Employment Doesn't Mean Work. Social Security Secures Socialism.* Quite frankly?'

'Not enormously.'

'I rather agree. Mrs Nelson thought of them last Sunday morning, while she was beating the Yorkshire. To cheer the country up at a stroke, you know, in place of strife.' He removed his trousers and Y-fronts, and draped them on the edge of his dressing-table. Mr Herbert Nelson was short and slight, with bright pink cheeks and bright blue eyes, scanty fair hair and a soft, finely wrinkled skin. He was always smiling. 'I'm in a bit of a hurry, I'm afraid,' he apologized. 'In five minutes I'm meeting some gnomes of Zurich, then I've got to join the cocktail circuit with some faceless bureaucrats of Brussels.'

'We need not be long.'

'I hope not. But if it's there, you'll catch it, won't you?' he asked anxiously.

In reply, Sir Lancelot snapped together a long, slim pair of surgical forceps in front of his own nose.

'It's most reassuring, your performing these regular examinations.' Mr Nelson lay on the bed. 'I could swear on the Bible there was one there, sometimes. Particularly in midsummer. And when the pollen count is high, naturally. I can even hear a buzz, quite distinctly. I turned to the Chancellor yesterday and asked if he could hear a buzz, too. I was most relieved when he couldn't, though quite frankly it seemed to fill the entire room. I suppose having a bee in one's bonnet is quite normal, but having a bee in one's – '

'Lie on your left side,' commanded Sir Lancelot. He took from his case a long, narrow glittering tube with a handle at one end. 'Easy now.'

'Oh, I'm perfectly used to it. I find it not unpleasant, in fact. Can you see the bee?'

'Not for the moment.'

'It never stings, you know. Just buzzes about.'

'By the way,' remarked Sir Lancelot, choosing his moment. 'You know of the trouble at St Swithin's?'

'Yes, I heard you were having some little local difficulties with your social contract. What is it? People who've never had it so good wanting it rather better? Jobs for all, the sack for nobody, a fatter pay packet every Christmas? It's the same everywhere, you know. Even among ordinary, decent working-class people. The doctrine of full employment only works without trouble among the Saints. Sure you can't see the bee?'

'I'm still looking,' said Sir Lancelot, applying his eye. 'I wondered if you might consider personal intervention? After all, we do an enormous export trade in the private part of St Swithin's. I'm sure the hospital deserves the Queen's Award for Industry, though perhaps the insignia on the door would look a little discouraging to arriving patients.'

'You want me to have a gritty confrontation with this Mr Crisps, or whoever he is? Make him feel the smack of firm Government?' continued Mr Nelson, half into his pillow. 'Get him to call off the strike at a stroke?'

'He's a very impressionable young man. From my own experience of him as a medical student, a little skilful bullying will bring him to heel.'

'Very well,' Mr Nelson agreed. 'I'll see him tonight, then. Nine o'clock? Then they'll have the film clips in good time for *The News At Ten*. No bee?'

'You're absolutely bee-free, take it from me,' said Sir Lancelot, withdrawing his instrument.

'Well, that's certainly a great relief. It always is, every time you stick your little scope in and look. Yet on occasions I could imagine I'd a whole hive up there. When we were at one of those Oriental embassies last week they offered me a ceremonial gift of honey. Mrs Nelson had to laugh. Their Ambassador wondered why, and got a bit shirty.'

He reached for his trousers. 'Excuse me. The wind of change. Tell me, Sir Lancelot. Do you think that I am perhaps a shade abnormal, imagining that I have bees buzzing about up there? I mean, a man in my position. Not that I should ever have any intention of resigning, of course.'

'Bizarre delusions involving animal or insect life are not unusual in great men,' Sir Lancelot reassured him, washing his hands in the adjoining small bathroom. 'Sir Winston Churchill sometimes had the feeling of being followed by a large black dog.'

'There's no known remedy, I suppose?' Mr Nelson pulled the trousers on.

'It is a condition admittedly resistant to treatment,' Sir Lancelot admitted. 'I had a similar case, much more severe than yours, who got himself into the most peculiar contortions by insisting on feeling for his bee with his fingertip. I exhorted him to pull his finger out. In the end, I was obliged to administer a general anaesthetic and assure him afterwards that I had performed a successful apisectomy – as I suppose the surgical removal of bees should be correctly termed.'

'That effected a permanent cure?'

'Alas, no. I shortly discovered the patient in exactly the same contorted position. He explained that having been put to such trouble ridding himself of the insect, he was keeping the route blocked in case it tried to get back. I shall tell young Chipps to present himself at nine sharp.'

The interview with Pip that evening was not the brightest bloom in Mr Nelson's convoluted garland of successful negotiations. As the pair sat down in the official reception room, the tail-coated butler placed at Pip's elbow a silver tray bearing a covered silver dish and a bottle of brown ale.

'Beer and sandwiches,' explained Mr Nelson in the armchair opposite. 'They're a traditional offering for these sort of late night, last minute, strike-averting talks. The employers' side get whisky, but it's the same principle.'

'I'm not very hungry or thirsty at the moment, I'm afraid,' said Pip, who refused to be dutifully impressed with his surroundings.

'Mrs Nelson can wrap them up, and you can enjoy them later,' he said kindly. 'Well, lad. What's the trouble? Trying to fight the Three Day Week War all over again?'

'I only want justice.'

'That's right, lad,' he agreed encouragingly. 'So do we all. By gum, we do. The lifeblood of democracy, that is.'

'I represent the reasonable aspirations of the down-trodden proletariat.'

'Have a fag.'

'Don't smoke, thanks.'

'Neither do I. Except cigars. And these days it doesn't do to go round in public with a big fat cigar in your face. Not like the times of Sir Winston Churchill. Always with his cigar, and his top hat, and his big black dog,' he continued fondly. 'Ah, you missed something during the war, lad. Mind, it was terrible with the bombs and that, and people being killed. I fought all the way through it you know,' he added with a note of defiant pride. 'As an Air Raid Warden. Bit of medical trouble kept me out of the Army. But the great spirit in the country! The Dunkirk spirit, the Alamein spirit, the spirit that cheerfully accepted shortages, rationing, the blackout, sing-songs down the shelters…' He hummed a few bars of *We'll Meet Again*. 'We were one big happy family in those days, lad. It was our finest hour. I call for us all, lad, to relive that hour now, whatever the sacrifice, whatever the inconvenience. Well, that's settled then,' he said, holding out his hand and rising.

'What's settled?'

'The strike, lad. You'll call it off in the national interest.'

'I certainly won't,' Pip said resentfully. 'Not after all the work I've put into it. I've hardly had a wink of sleep since last Tuesday.'

'You young lads don't need a lot of sleep, not like we old codgers,' continued Mr Nelson in a kindly voice, giving the impression of being about to nod off in his chair. 'I remember when I was your age, lad. Not sleeping more than an hour a night for months on end. Sweating in the factory seven days a week, just to make a few bob to keep my poor old mum. By gum, we northerners were tough in those days. I went to work barefoot. Nothing to eat all day but bread and marge. They're not like that back in Barnet any more, I'll wager. I've been through it all, lad. I know how ordinary working folk feel. It's time to put our shoulders to the wheel with the broadest backs bearing the greatest burden. So call off your strike, lad. Let our first job be getting Britain back to work.'

'No,' said Pip.

'You got a mother still this side of Heaven, lad? Old age pension, I suppose? Senior Citizens, they call them these days. To me, they were just Gran and Pop.' He wiped an eye delicately from a convenient box of tissues at his elbow. 'They're the folk who suffer from a selfish minority grabbing wage rises. The old, the sick – the sick, you know all about the sick, lad – the handicapped, the underprivileged, the homeless, the poor, and so on.'

'But those are exactly the people I'm trying to benefit,' Pip objected. 'Improving their care by keeping their doctors in the country, and stopping medical energies being lavished on a few privileged patients.'

'Well, lad, I've got some ambassador bloke to see, so I'll have to send you on your way.' Mr Nelson glanced at his watch, seeing that the three minutes allowed for the interview had expired. 'Let's keep the lines and the options open. Any time you change your mind, give us a phone call. I'm always available. Servant of the People. Sure you don't want your beer and sandwiches? Know your way out? Don't hear a buzzing noise, do you?'

'Not at all.'

'Ah, it must have escaped this afternoon. We'll keep in touch,' he said with crushing finality.

On the doorstep, Pip was met with television cameras, clicking lenses, jabbing microphones.

'The strike goes on,' he announced, wrapping his coat tightly round him. 'I call upon our brother trade unionists in the entire country to back one hundred per cent the struggle of the workers in the Health Service.'

'You're demanding a general strike?' asked a man with a microphone.

'Am I?' Pip scratched his head. 'Yes, I suppose I must be. Definitely.'

Another man asked, 'But supposing the trade union movement as a whole doesn't respond?'

'That's a very good question.' Pip stood on the doorstep, nodding thoughtfully until the solution came to him. 'ACHE will simply stop even emergencies being treated in any hospital.'

'But, Mr Chipps,' cried someone else. 'Isn't that the mentality of the hijacker?'

Pip gave a smile. 'Exactly. And hijackers are the only practical politicians today who know exactly what they want and almost always get it. It isn't their fault that they threaten to blow aeroplanes and so on to little bits. It's the fault of modern civilization. Life has grown quite ridiculously complicated. Hasn't that occurred to you? Anyone can get their own way, if they know precisely where to seek it. It takes such a very small spanner to jam the works, and anyone who rocks the boat has his hand on the tiller,' he ended a little confusedly. 'Now if you'll excuse me, my strike committee are waiting in the Mini.'

# 19

Just before ten o'clock the following morning, a Saturday of brilliant June sunshine which beguiled the nation's darkest hour since the war, the matron of the Bertram Bunn Wing sat at the desk in her hot, un-air-conditioned steel-and-glass office, looking gloomily at the front page of a tabloid newspaper.

ALL OUT – OR THE MORGUE,

said the big headline.

The front page was filled with the photograph of a wild-eyed Pip, giving a double clenched-fist salute on the doorstep the previous evening. The story in heavy type said,

> *Supermilitant shop steward Pip called for a general strike yesterday to support ACHE's action against private patients and dodging doctors. And a grim alternative – ACHE will black even emergency cases.*
>
> *TUC chiefs – gathered for gala opening of Yorkshire's multi-million pound working men's club with draught champagne and double-shift striptease – declared the strike call needed 'Serious consideration'. A Government spokesman described the situation as 'Extremely delicate, if not rather desperate'. The £ plummeted overnight AND England lost the Test Match in two days AND the weather forecast says WET and STORMY! So cheer up! BRITAIN CAN BLOODY WELL TAKE IT!*

'Grinning and bearing,' sighed the matron to herself. 'The great British virtue. Or the great British stupidity?'

Emotions as warm and entangled as a plate of spaghetti lay within her breast as she continued staring at the page. She could not entirely suppress a feeling of pride that her nephew was sunning himself in the spotlights of fame. After all, none of the family had ever before got their picture in the papers, apart from Pip's mother with the vicar in the *Wiveliscombe Bugle*. But Pip was thoroughly frightening. He was like some fondly indulged, playfully destructive puppy who had developed rabies. He really deserved putting down, she decided, if in some unhurtful way. The matron frowned, searching her mind for the fate of other turbulent pests. She supposed they ended up immured in the House of Lords, and Pip was perhaps a little young for that.

She opened the newspaper. The emotions behind the severely cut bosom of her uniform instantly straightened themselves out. The page facing her was filled with a photograph of Sir Lancelot Spratt's patient — her top half, smiling winsomely from her bath upstairs in the Bertram Bunn Wing, while daintily sponging the nape of her neck.

### BLACKLEG BRENDA!

it said beneath. The caption went on,

> *Actress Brenda Bristols, strikebound since Tuesday night in St Swithin's Hospital private wing, serves meals and cleans floors and aids the nurses — and nobody objects! Said Brenda, tubbing after a hard day's work. 'All the hospitalized sheikhs want to take their money out of Britain because of the crisis. But they can't. The private patients' telephones are on strike!'*

'Serves meals! Cleans floors!' muttered the matron. 'She doesn't do a hand's turn, except when there's a photographer about. That woman's clothes come on and off quicker than the television commercials, and probably just as often.'

She continued glaring at the photograph. She found inconceivable the attention, the courtesy, the interest which Sir Lancelot lavished on such a mammary monstrosity. Particularly as the matron had discovered from Tony Havens' case notes that Brenda Bristols' real name was Elaine

Fishwick and that she had been a Wimpy Bar waitress in Slough and divorced three times. The sort of woman to console Sir Lancelot in his widowhood, she reflected, should be entirely different. Serious minded, intelligent, energetic, reliable, with much conversation in common by way of interesting operations, symptoms, and diseased organs.

The matron sat back, drumming her delicate fingertips slowly against the edge of her desk. She had not played her cards right the previous evening, she had to admit. Worse still, she had wrongly accused Sir Lancelot of revoking. But the game was not over. Brenda Bristols would be excluded from the play, once this ridiculous strike of Pip's was over, if it did not end up in Civil War II.

There was a knock.

She pushed the newspaper into a desk drawer. 'Come in.'

Lord Hopcroft appeared, fully dressed. 'Good morning, Matron. I was just leaving.'

She pursed her lips. 'I don't remember giving permission for your discharge?'

'No, you didn't. The computer discharged me.'

'I see. Well, I hope your stay was comfortable. As comfortable as possible under these unruly circumstances.'

'I have not a word of criticism, Matron. Everyone was absolutely marvellous.'

'Thank you,' she said, the frost fading slightly.

'I've come to collect them.'

'Collect what?'

'The twins.'

The matron frowned. 'Are they your relatives?'

'Most definitely. I had them late last night. Two girls, according to the computer.'

'But there must be some mistake –'

'Not a bit. The computer cannot make mistakes. You told me as much yourself, repeatedly. Well, where have you got them?' he asked, smiling round the room. 'I just can't wait to bring them home. My butler will be terribly thrilled. He is rather on the effeminate side.'

'Lord Hopcroft,' she addressed him severely. 'You were perhaps diagnosed by the computer as having *delusions* you'd given birth to twin girls.'

'I'm not having delusions,' he returned firmly. 'The computer may be having delusions, but that's no affair of mine. I'm in quite a tizzy deciding what to call them. One must be so careful not labelling girls with trendy names. They do so date. A friend of my former wife christened her little one "Twiggy", which I'm sure may be something of a mistake. What shall I feed them on, Matron? Putting the babies to the breast would seem to present certain technical difficulties.'

'I always advise my mothers to attempt breastfeeding, at the very least. It's so much more satisfying.'

'One could but try, I suppose,' he mused.

'If there isn't enough natural milk, then you will find any of the proprietary artificial feeds perfectly satisfactory.'

'How often should one give them?'

'I recommend feeding on demand. That is so much more natural than giving your baby meals at fixed intervals. Its little stomach may not be at all ready. Weaning of course, particularly in the case of twins – What am I telling you all this for?' she broke off crossly. 'Of course you haven't had twin babies. You haven't had even one.'

'But the computer print-out gave their weights, their blood-groups, their genetic details – '

The matron silenced him with a firm tap of her pencil on the desk. 'We shall forward your twins to your home address.'

'Like buying things at Fortnum and Mason's,' he agreed amiably. 'Yes, having them delivered would certainly be more convenient. I hope my chauffeur is still waiting. He will be needing a shave rather badly by now, poor fellow. Again, Matron, thank you. I had such an easy and painless confinement. I shall certainly make a point of bearing the rest of my family in your hospital. And it was quite an excitement to meet Brenda Bristols in the flesh.'

'You think so?' The ice reformed.

'She is coming to convalesce at a little shack I own near St Tropez, once Sir Lancelot has nipped that lump from her breast. A ridiculously small one for an operation, it seemed to me. But I suppose all things are relative.

Oh, just one final matter,' he remembered. 'The computer tells me to obtain my maternity grant. Where do I apply for that?'

'I should try the administrators' office in the main St Swithin's building,' she told him bleakly. 'Unless they are all on strike.'

As Lord Hopcroft left, a second visitor pushed hastily into the office past him. He was slight, slim and sandy-haired, drooping-moustached, bright-eyed and fresh complexioned. He wore a crumpled brown suit of Donegal tweed, and carried a shapeless tweed hat with fishing flies round the brim.

'Florence –'

She jerked upright in her chair. 'Horace –'

'What *is* Pip up to?' he asked at once.

'I don't know. Trying to take over Downing Street as he's already taken over St Swithin's, it seems.'

'And Buckingham Palace into the bargain. I can't understand it. He always used to shy away from responsibility. He even refused to become Secretary of his mother's Poetry Circle.'

Dr Horace Chipps sat down, staring at his brown-booted feet.

'You saw his antics on television these last two nights?' asked the matron.

'Yes. That's why I decided I must come up to London. I wanted to look at a new trout rod in Farlow's, anyway,' he added. 'It's dreadfully worrying about Pip. Is he suffering from mania? Ought he to be shut away somewhere? I know he wanted to be a psychiatrist, an ambition I always suspect to be a symptom of incipient mental disease. But what's he doing as a porter, anyway? Why isn't he pursuing his medical studies?'

'I'm afraid his medical studies have raced out of sight. He was expelled after failing his exams.'

'That happened to me dozens of times,' Dr Chipps dismissed the incident. 'I simply turned up again at the start of the next session as if nothing had happened. Nobody said anything. They always feel dreadfully foolish expelling a St Swithin's man – who the hospital naturally recognize as the best all-round top-quality students in London.'

'It's simply that Pip has got into the hands of the wrong people.'

'Who?'

'Faith Lychfield.'

'The dean's daughter?' he asked in amazement. 'But I met her on their holidays in Somerset. She's a sweet and charming little girl who couldn't say boo to a gosling.'

'Young people do peculiar and most unexpected things these days. The sons and daughters of even highly respectable families frequently become hippies, drop-outs, drug addicts, alcoholics, sex maniacs and so on.' The matron added with a hard look, 'Personally, I put the blame on the parents.'

'I suppose you're suggesting that I brought up Pip wrongly?' he said, returning her glare. 'Well, I didn't. I taught him cricket at ten and fly-fishing at fourteen. How to deliver lambs at fifteen and how to classify butterflies at sixteen. At seventeen how to train gundogs, and at eighteen how to drink scrumpy without being sick.' Dr Chipps stood up. 'I'd better have a word with my son, I suppose,' he decided. 'Before they start calling out the Army and Navy, if we've got much of either left. Where can I find him?'

'His usual haunt is the porters' room in St Swithin's basement.'

'I shall never find my way about my own hospital, now it's been so extravagantly rebuilt,' he complained sadly.

'Just follow the picket lines, and you'll get right to the spot,' she advised him crisply.

The front of St Swithin's struck Dr Horace Chipps as resembling a film unit on location rather than a hospital forecourt. There were cameras, lights, cables and large vans everywhere. Bright-shirted men strode decisively about, pointing in all directions. Girls in jeans and enormous glasses hurried after them attentively with notebooks and stopwatches. Men dangling with cameras or festooned with microphones lolled comfortably in the warm sunshine. He noticed, looking equally lost, the pinkish, smartly dressed man who had left the matron's office as he had entered it.

They caught each other's eye. 'Excuse me,' said the stranger to Dr Chipps. 'I'm looking for the administrators' office. I've just been discharged from hospital.'

'Nothing serious, I hope?' the doctor asked kindly.

'Not at all. I have given birth to twins.'

Dr Chipps blinked. Not only St Swithin's but medicine had been startlingly modernized since his own student days. He looked round. A young man in Highland dress was holding up a placard saying, HOME RULE FOR CLYDESIDE. Nearer stood a brown-coated youth, gloomily bearing aloft the message FAIR CURES FOR ALL. 'Certainly, Guv'nor, first floor,' he replied politely, when Lord Hopcroft asked for directions.

'And what's your opinion of the dispute?'

'Of the what?'

'The strike.'

'Oh, that. Ain't thought, really.'

'But surely,' suggested Lord Hopcroft gently, 'you understand *why* you're on strike?'

'Oh, yes. I'm on strike because we was called out.'

'But do you know *why* you were called out?'

'The shop steward called us out.'

'Exactly. But for what reasons did your shop steward decide this?'

'Look, Guv, I ain't a bleedin' professor.'

Lord Hopcroft reached the first floor offices. They were deserted, except for a young man in a bright T-shirt and jeans, visible through a far door shovelling papers into a brief-case. 'Are you on strike, too?' Lord Hopcroft asked, approaching.

The young man looked up. 'Not on Saturday. We never do anything on Saturdays. I'm clearing up. I've been fired. Just because I blew a few quid of hospital funds on some German bird in a classy restaurant. It's damn unfair. I'd call a strike over it, if there wasn't one on already.'

'What job are you going to do instead?' Lord Hopcroft asked sympathetically.

'Not another hospital,' Mr Grout said feelingly. 'Not where you can't even wear decent gear, and have to be on your dignity all day. I'm going to try hotels. Hotels are just the same as hospitals, anyway. Except that fewer people die in them.'

Lord Hopcroft snapped his fingers. 'By God! I think you've given me the answer, young man. My company owns a couple of modern hotels in central London doing atrociously badly at the moment. But they've got an efficient and – I flatter myself – most contented staff. The cooking and cellar are all that the most fastidious capitalist or caliph might desire. I could easily knock a few suites into rooms for the doctors to do whatever they do in them. After all, an operating theatre seems to me only a rather elaborate bathroom. I'll get one of the top couturiers to design the nurses' uniforms,' he continued enthusiastically. 'Nosegays and things, get rid of this dreadful butch Florence Nightingale image. There will never be any industrial trouble, because the domestic staff will be accepted as having an interest in their pockets rather than their patients. Why should it be otherwise? We are surely past the days when monks and nuns toiled to bring the sick their possets and so on? A great pity, in a way,' he reflected. 'They were a splendid source of cheap labour. Henry the Eighth has much to answer for.'

'You need a licence,' Mr Grout pointed out gloomily. 'Under the Public Health Act, 1936, Sections one hundred and eighty-seven to one-nine-five.'

'What precisely was the job you lost?'

'Junior administrator. As a matter of fact, all this trouble's due to me.' He nodded towards the crowded forecourt. 'I was the one who gave Chipps his job as a porter. Only last Tuesday.'

'You obviously have a flair for picking the coming man,' Lord Hopcroft complimented him. 'I may well have room for you in my new scheme. Would you care to join me for lunch in one of my hotels? Then you can come along and help me smash up our office computer. I have reason to suspect they can be unreliable instruments.'

# 20

'Do you mind slipping out of the mortuary entrance under cover of this hearse, Dad?' Pip was conducting Dr Chipps from the rear of St Swithin's, the same time as Lord Hopcroft was leaving the front door with Mr Grout. 'I'll get mobbed if I show my face at the main entrance.'

'In the old St Swithin's building,' his father reflected fondly, 'the mortuary was the only route into the Nurses' Home after midnight. I'm sure it was splendid training for the girls in the realities of their chosen profession, once you'd pushed them over the gate.'

'Where should we go for this drink?'

'I wonder if the Cock and Feathers still stands?' his father suggested. Pip frowned, trying to remember. 'It was a favourite among the students in my day. It should be just along this alley, as I recall. Though of course I haven't been back to London more than a couple of times since I qualified.'

'It was good of you to come and see me today, Dad.'

'I thought I'd look you up,' he explained casually. 'It's interesting to see you in your natural habitat. There's the pub.'

'Seems to be one I've overlooked,' Pip confessed.

'It hasn't changed a bit. Though I'm afraid that little red-headed barmaid will have changed considerably.'

They pushed through the narrow doorway of a small, grimy pub, seemingly too insignificant for the baleful notice of the planners who had savagely redesigned the area. The sign overhead was faded, the single window giving into the public bar was unwashed, the interior was dim, empty, sawdust-floored and smelling strongly of beer in all stages of decomposition.

'Morning, Horace,' said a fat man in shirtsleeves and braces behind the bar. 'Your usual?'

'Please.'

'You haven't been in for some time.'

'No. I've been living in Somerset.'

'Nice down there?' The man started drawing a pint.

'Very nice.'

'It must be getting on for…what? Twenty years?'

'Nearer thirty, Sam.'

'Time flies, dunnit?'

'It certainly does.'

'Seems like yesterday. Same for your friend?'

'He's my son.'

'Don't say? Yes, time does fly,' the publican observed reflectively.

Dr Chipps took his son to a bench and a rough table in one corner. 'Do you see, Pip? Once you've been a student at St Swithin's, that's not something you can wipe out of your life like some holiday you once enjoyed. The hospital isn't just some modern technical school, turning out doctors who are simply garage mechanics for human beings. Though admittedly, that's what the place now looks like,' he conceded. 'The buildings may be brand-new, but as an institution St Swithin's has been going strong over four hundred years. And a bit of that history sticks to all of us.'

'Perhaps I should have been more appreciative of my hospital if it hadn't thrown me out,' Pip objected mildly.

'Some of the most zealous of St Swithin's enthusiasts are its failed students. They look back on it as a sunny forcing-ground before they found success in other fields.'

'Well, I've found success in another field.'

'Only by trying to destroy St Swithin's and everything it stands for,' his father pointed out.

Pip sipped his pint. 'It's exactly that I'm proud of.'

'That's only your opinion,' his father told him forbearingly.

'I'm unshakeably convinced it's the right one.'

'What could you tell jesting Pilate? That the truth is only a point of view. Though I suppose black and white are the same thing to a blind man, and in my experience of humanity most people are pretty wall-eyed. That's why they're so easily pushed about by strongly minded and noisy activists. Like you.'

'May I tell you what, in my eyes, St Swithin's stands for? Starkly clearly?'

'I think I've gathered that already from the papers. Private practice and doctors' emigration. Both of which you are determined to stop. By allowing coronaries and appendices and haemorrhages and so on to die through lack of treatment.'

'I was a little carried away by my own words at that particular point,' Pip admitted shamefacedly.

'I don't suppose anyone took you too seriously,' his father told him easily. 'The country's pretty used to trade union braggarts who enjoy making the public's flesh creep on television.'

'Dad, you've only diagnosed the symptoms of my argument against St Swithin's. Not the condition that's causing me to form them. I really object to something more fundamental. To doctors setting themselves up as something special, as people way above their fellow workers in the National Health Service.'

His father nodded. 'Very well. Shall we become even more fundamental than that? Who is the only special person in any hospital?'

'The patient,' Pip answered promptly.

'And don't you see, Pip, how the doctor at the bedside is the most important person that patient will ever know in his entire life? Just for those few minutes of his consultation, the doctor becomes more important than the patient's wife and children. More important than his boss, certainly more than his Prime Minister. And if I may say so, more important than any hospital porter.'

The pub remained empty. The man in braces stood behind his beer-taps staring at the pair, but from habit blind and deaf and lost in thoughts of his own – which he had long ago told Dr Chipps he discovered vastly more entertaining than the conversations of his customers.

'That's not a rôle the doctor seeks,' Pip's father continued. 'Doctors are humble people, despite the jokes against them. Anyone must be humble, who's picked to bits the corpse of a fellow human and seen what a ridiculously frail thing it is. We wear our importance for exactly the same reason as we do most other things in our lives. Directly or indirectly to help our patients. Our raw material is the defenceless human body, our stock in trade is life and death. We doctors are different, and we've got to stay different.'

Pip sipped his tankard of beer for some moments in silence. Then he gave a smile, and suggested pleasantly, 'I know how all this is ending up. Imploring me, as my father, to call off the strike.'

'Only advising you to. The doctor can but advise, the decision is always the patient's, even if it's to let himself die. And sometimes the patient is the wiser of the two. But you could become the most popular man in the country by ten o'clock tonight, Pip. If you'd be the first union leader to stand up on television and say, "We're going back to work. Now I've had a chance to think things over, I can see quite clearly that we were in the wrong." Everyone in the Kingdom is heartily fed up with union bullying, I can assure you of that. And anyway, hospitals are the very last places for the exercise of trade union power politics. You're only hurting people who are sore enough already.'

'It's not quite so simple,' Pip objected. 'I've my members of ACHE to think of. I would never break faith with them. They'd never forgive me if I did.'

'You talk as though your members had a more binding relationship to you than to the Queen,' said his father more shortly.

'Perhaps they have? The trade unions are a state within our State. They enjoy first call on the loyalty of their members, who are far more scared of breaking union solidarity than they are of breaking the Law of the land. That's because simple individuals feel hopelessly inadequate and unprotected in the face of our complex modern society. If you want to solve the trade union problem, Dad,' Pip added with a grin, 'you've got to go back to the Middle Ages and start again in a different direction.'

'Well, think over all I've said.' Dr Chipps drained his tankard. 'My train leaves Paddington in an hour.'

'So soon? I haven't got a watch.'

'You don't need one in the city, where the passage of time screams at you every minute. Only in the country, where it simply gets light and gets dark. I must be back for my special surgery on Saturday evening. It's for the psychologically distressed, the depressives, the insomniacs, the hysterics, the plain unhappy, the people you just mentioned who can't cope with modern life. I make time at weekends to sit and talk to them. I could pack them off to a psychiatrist in hospital, but I think the family doctor works rather better. After all, I know these patients pretty well. I try to sustain the doctor's traditional rôle with them – a friend in health, a saviour in sickness, a companion in death. A lot of practitioners busier than me dish out tranquillizers and barbiturates by the shovelful. But I believe that my personality is less toxic than drugs, and less likely to result in death from an overdose. Besides, it's the best of the fishing season,' he ended, 'and I might manage an hour on the river at dusk.'

'But you've time for another pint?'

'Always.' Dr Chipps raised the tankard. ' "Then to the spicy nut-brown ale." I do wish your mother could write lines like that.'

At that same moment, Sir Lancelot Spratt was driving westwards from his Harley Street consulting rooms towards the City, beside him in the Rolls one of his patients.

'It's a great relief, I must say,' Sir Lancelot's companion remarked thankfully. 'Getting the bandage off at last. Five days is a long time to see absolutely nothing of the world about you.'

'You kept it on religiously, did you, Alfred? And indulged in absolutely no activity?'

'I always obey doctors' orders. I've a high respect for the medical profession. And you can't complain that I don't show it in a practical way.'

'Indeed. Not many of my patients would come along regularly twice a year to the examinations, and allow the students to test their brains upon them. I only hope it's support which the medical profession won't lose after your last experience?'

'Oh, there's nutcases about everywhere these days,' the patient said accommodatingly. 'Don't you worry, Lancelot, it takes more than that to put a bloke like me off. Though having only one eye in the first place, it was admittedly a bit scary at the time. I must say, you did a fine job on the damage. But it was a bit hard trying to pick up all this fuss you're having at St Swithin's only from lying on my back listening to the radio bulletins. I itched to read a paper or watch the telly.'

'I didn't really want to expose the eye for another week,' Sir Lancelot informed him, driving well over the speed limit along almost empty Saturday morning City streets. 'You seem to have recovered pretty well, but I fancy I was very wise to keep it out of action.'

'Better find if I can sort things out in your hospital, I suppose,' said his passenger gloomily. 'Though now I can see, I was hoping to get away for some golf.'

'Wasn't there anyone on your union's executive, Alfred, who would have taken action about St Swithin's while you were *hors de combat*?'

'The whole lot's off on a special charter flight to Barbados. I'll have it sorted out in a jiffy, don't you worry. This bloke everyone's talking about. Chipps. Must be some screwy hothead. Bane of my life, that lot. And of every other fair-minded and decent union official in the land. They're always stirring it up. No wonder they say that the country's ungovernable. What do you expect, when any hairy twit with a loud enough voice can get sensible men to listen? I reckon the country's simply losing its sense of humour.'

'We have not yet quite reached that ultimate disaster. Though I would agree with you and the late E M Forster – whose works I am reading in bed – that what the world needs today are such negative virtues as *not* being huffy, touchy, irritable or revengeful. Positive ideas always seem to get so many people hurt or killed, or if they're particularly lucky locked up.'

Sir Lancelot stopped his car outside the mortuary entrance at the rear of St Swithin's. 'You'll find Mr Pip Chipps down in the porters' room, Alfred. That's in the basement. You'll excuse me if I leave you to it? I've a case waiting operation in the Clinic.'

'Thanks for the lift. See you at the golf club.'

The long, lean form of Alfred Dimchurch left the Rolls and made its way into the hospital and down the stairs. He remembered the route to the porters' room in the basement. He pushed the door open. In the smoke-streaked atmosphere stood a small knot of brown-coated men, a pretty, fair girl, the well-recognized Harold Sapworth, and a young man in the act of addressing them from a bench.

'In inaugurating this splendid dartboard,' Pip was declaiming, 'which apparently has for some months been tucked into the back of Mr Grout's desk upstairs, I ask you, Brothers, to see it not as a gift, but as an absolute and minimal right which justly demanded – '

He was interrupted by a noise like a tiger awaking from a bad dream. 'You!' demanded the visitor. 'What the hell are you doing here?'

'Me? I'm Pip Chipps, of course.'

'Chipps? Chipps? You? You walking case of grievous bodily harm? You murderous maniac? You madman who goes round trying to blind people for life – '

'And what are *you* doing here, may I ask?' inquired Pip, recovering his dignity. 'As far as I'm concerned, you're an examination patient. I agree, I made a misdiagnosis in your case. That can happen to the cleverest of doctors. I apologized at the time, if you remember. You now seem none the worse for your experience. I don't see why you should come hounding me down here to complain. I'm a very busy man. As you ought to know, if you read your newspapers.'

'I'll tell you what I'm doing here, laddie. I'm Alfred Dimchurch. I'm President of ACHE, that's who I am. And I expel you from the union forthwith,' he thundered.

Pip gazed quickly round. 'You can't.'

'Oh yes, I can. I can expel anyone I like. Look in the rule book. Not that I expect you've so much as laid hands on it. If only I'd had my sight these last five days, and seen who was causing this childish trouble – '

'Brothers! Comrades!' Pip threw open his arms, standing on the bench. 'Lend me your ears. You have seen the terrible injustices existing in this hospital. You have seen the vile iniquities of its doctors. You have seen, too, my fight against both. Brothers, this is no time to lose your commander. Not in the heat of battle, with victory in our grasp, the smell of our enemies' blood on our boots. No, it is the moment from which I am confident of leading you to the utter rout of capitalism itself. You would not want me to desert my troops, would you? Whatever this old buffer says, I shall stay. I shall not break faith with my valiant army. On, on! Once more unto the picket line, dear brothers. Cry "God for Harold! England and St Swithin's!" '

Pip's speech was met with a sound new to the orator's ears. A raspberry. He looked down. It originated from Harold Sapworth.

'I beg your pardon?' Pip asked, pained.

'Stow it, mate. We've heard all that before.'

'I was only asking you to carry on with the strike. I thought the burden of my words pretty clear.'

'The strike's off, mate.'

Pip gazed unbelievingly. 'I gave no orders to that effect.'

Harold sucked the tip of his thumb. 'Nothing to do with you, mate. You're nothing to do with us either, mate.'

'But I'm your friend,' Pip protested hotly.

'We got a closed shop here at St Swithin's. You ain't a union member any longer. So you'd better hop it double quick, afore we take what you might call appropriate action, that is, putting the old boot in.'

'How dare you,' said Pip, turning pink.

'And what's all this here, then?' Harold Sapworth produced some closely written sheets of paper from the pocket of his own coat. 'What I found in that geezer Grout's desk, when he sent me up to collect the dartboard this morning. Your writing, ain't it?' he asked Pip threateningly. 'Scheme for making a hundred of your mates down here redundant.'

'Some shop steward,' snorted Alfred Dimchurch.

'Bleeding scab, rather,' Harold Sapworth agreed.

To a fanfare of hostile noises, Pip said furiously to Harold Sapworth, taking off his brown coat, 'I've a damn good mind to thump you one.'

'Wouldn't if I was you, mate. You're well outnumbered. Even forgetting our President, who may be a bit past handing out a bunch of fives. Don't want to end up in the hospital, do you? Wouldn't have a very comfortable stay there, either, if you asks me.'

Pip threw his coat savagely to the concrete floor. 'I'm damned if I'm giving in without a fight, you uneducated Judas.'

Then it happened again. Faith slipped her hand in his. He stopped.

'Pip, love,' she said quietly. 'It is far, far wiser to fight another day. By then, you see, nobody may be feeling like it.'

# 21

'My dear Josephine,' said the dean of St Swithin's to his wife, as he relaxed in the bow-windowed parlour of his house in Lazar Row just after six o'clock that evening. 'This definitely calls for a celebration. Fetch some sherry. Reach deep into my shoe cupboard upstairs for a bottle of the very old *cuvée* Butler. That really was an excellent year.'

He lay stretched in his deep armchair, humming and beating his fingertips together delightedly. There was a flash outside, a crash of thunder and the rain began to hose down. The break in the splendid week's weather had arrived as foreseen by the morning's paper. It caused the dean only to break out reedily from *The Mikado*, ' "The threatened cloud has passed away, And brightly shines the dawning day." ' He had always fancied himself at amateur theatricals.

As Josephine returned with the dusty bottle and three glasses, he continued cheerfully, 'St Swithin's can breathe again. The country can breathe again. We are all back to square one. Exactly where we were sitting comfortably before that adolescent agitator ran amok. The trouble I've been put to! The worry I've suffered! At last we can get on with our proper work of being doctors, not industrial conciliators. Who's the third glass for?' he asked sharply.

'Faith, of course. She'll be in soon. She phoned to say she's home for the weekend.'

'I don't know how Faith dare show her face in the house.'

'Lionel, you really can't talk like that about your own daughter. You should anyway be in a magnanimous mood all round. That's what Winston Churchill advised any victor.'

The faint scowl which had congealed on the dean's brow evaporated. 'Yes, I agree. I'm simply relieved that the horrible nightmare is over. I'd no idea that Dimchurch was one of Lancelot's golfing partners. Lancelot certainly does keep strange company. I suppose it's understandable, nobody else in any civilized golf club would play with him. By the way, Lancelot's gone commercial.'

'I don't think I entirely follow,' Josephine said, pouring out two glasses of sherry.

'You heard the telephone just now? It was from Lord Hopcroft. The man who owns those outrageously expensive hotels. He charged me extra for coffee, if I remember. Quite outrageous. I always understood coffee to be an integral part of a gentleman's dinner –'

'Lord Hopcroft,' she interrupted. 'What did he say, dear?'

'Oh, yes. He's full of some idea about starting a luxurious private hospital in a converted hotel. He wants a medical council to take charge, on which Lancelot has already agreed to serve – naturally, the emoluments being somewhat hefty.'

His wife looked puzzled. 'Then why did you refuse, dear?'

The dean tapped his nose. 'I can be crafty. A place like that will never attract the same custom as the genuine article. By that I mean the Bertram Bunn Wing of St Swithin's Hospital, which I am now confidently going to enlarge and stick up the prices. The union will never dare risk making a fool of itself again for years and years. Old Dimchurch will wangle in some compliant shop steward, and we doctors can get away with murder. Good evening, Faith,' he added, as his daughter entered, looking solemn. 'Have some sherry. Its the *cuvée* Butler, which is to my mind superior even to the *cuvée* Heathcoat Amory, though that's a year with many interesting little features.'

'Daddy, I want you to reinstate Pip in the medical school.'

The dean jumped in his chair, accompanied by a roll of thunder. 'That snotty-nosed Stalin? That lecherous Lenin? Not, as his friend Mr Sapworth would say, on my bleeding nelly.'

'Daddy, you must try and be cerebral about this,' she advised. 'Pip's an awfully good student really, terribly intelligent and by nature enormously hardworking. He promised me to slave at his books, and he's sure to sail through the exam in December. Particularly if there aren't any one-eyed patients.'

The dean's hand quivered, holding out his empty glass to Josephine for a refill. 'Chipps himself put you up to this, didn't he? You are unhappily completely and disastrously in his power. Though what a girl like you can see in that hirsute Hitler, I can't imagine.'

'No, Daddy. I am asking only from my sense of fairness. Pip no longer means anything to me.'

'Kindly pull the other one, with the bells on.'

'Honestly. We've split up. For a while, at any rate. We decided this afternoon that our personalities are too powerful for each other. They seem to set off a chain reaction, like the atomic bomb.'

'I don't know what they set off last Monday night,' he told her severely, sipping his sherry.

'Last Monday night nothing happened.'

The dean gave a laugh, sounding like a stepped-on terrier. 'When a young man shacks up with a young woman, even if the shack in question happens to be a geriatric unit – '

'But poor Pip.' She paused. 'He was too ham-fisted. Besides, there wasn't much room.'

The dean grunted.

'A St Swithin's student and his evening's dancing companion,' murmured the dean's wife gently, '*have* been known to sleep the rest of the night in the same bed perfectly innocently.'

'I was simply too drunk,' commented the dean. 'I mean... But what about Tuesday night? Not to mention Wednesday, Thursday and Friday?' he demanded.

'We were far too busy, organizing his porters' scheme and then the strike.'

The dean gave a snort. There was another crash of thunder. 'Oh, very well, very well. I know I can believe my own daughter. Thank God, I brought you up with a proper sense of values. Tell him to report to the wards on Monday and keep entirely out of my sight until Christmas.'

'Thank you, Daddy.' Faith clasped her hands together, eyes sparkling. 'I knew you'd have no victimization.'

'I do wish you wouldn't use those awful trade union phrases. I hope that you will now take life seriously again, and do your proper duty to the world you live in.'

'You always taught me to do my duty, Daddy, without fear or favour.'

'I know there is plenty of good in you, Faith,' he added, holding out his empty glass again. 'After all, you are my daughter.'

'And mine,' said Josephine, filling it up.

'You can't have seen much of the destitute men this terrible week?'

'I had to give that job up, Daddy. It was only fair. But I've got a surprise. On Friday, Mr Clapper took me on as a social worker in St Swithin's itself.'

'But how absolutely splendid. Quite delightful. You and I, working upon the sick in the same hospital. Have some more sherry. How on earth did you manage it, without any influence from me?'

'I wanted to stand beholden to no man, Daddy. Not even to you.'

'Stout girl. Be independent. That's what I like to hear. Besides, it would have been no end of trouble, greasing up that awful buffoon Clapper.'

'I had to join ACHE, of course.'

The scowl reconstituted itself briefly on the dean's brow. 'Couldn't be helped, I suppose. Part of modern life.'

'I'm late home this evening, because of a meeting electing the new shop steward.'

'That little runt Harold Sapworth, I take it?'

'No, Daddy. Me. It was unanimous.'

The dean's glass smashed on the floor.

'As you always taught me, Daddy, I shall pursue my duties without obligation to, or intimidation from, anyone. At nine on Monday morning I'd like to see you in the Bertie Bunn, please. I want to put to you the union's new rules for restrictions on private patients. You may find it a somewhat painful operation, Daddy, but one which I am afraid you must submit to.'

There was a roll of thunder. 'Josephine,' said the dean. 'Drink.'

'More sherry, dear?'

'No. Brandy. Right at the back of my shoe cupboard there's a bottle of the *cuvée* Churchill. It's pre-war, my father bought it in 1940 to see us through the blitz. We hear enough about the Dunkirk spirit. Now I'm going to consume it. Fetch me a large tumbler.'

# RICHARD GORDON

## DOCTOR IN THE HOUSE

Richard Gordon's acceptance into St Swithin's medical school came as no surprise to anyone, least of all him – after all, he had been to public school, played first XV rugby, and his father was, let's face it, 'a St Swithin's man'. Surely he was set for life. It was rather a shock then to discover that, once there, he would actually have to work, and quite hard. Fortunately for Richard Gordon, life proved not to be all dissection and textbooks after all… This hilarious hospital comedy is perfect reading for anyone who's ever wondered exactly what medical students get up to in their training. Just don't read it on your way to the doctor's!

'Uproarious, extremely iconoclastic' – *Evening News*
'A delightful book' – *Sunday Times*

## DOCTOR AT SEA

Richard Gordon's life was moving rapidly towards middle-aged lethargy – or so he felt. Employed as an assistant in general practice – the medical equivalent of a poor curate – and having been 'persuaded' that marriage is as much an obligation for a young doctor as celibacy for a priest, Richard sees the rest of his life stretching before him. Losing his nerve, and desperately in need of an antidote, he instead signs on with the Fathom Steamboat Company. What follows is a hilarious tale of nautical diseases and assorted misadventures at sea. Yet he also becomes embroiled in a mystery – what is in the Captain's stomach remedy? And more to the point, what on earth happened to the previous doctor?

'Sheer unadulterated fun' – *Star*

# Richard Gordon

## Doctor at Large

Dr Richard Gordon's first job after qualifying takes him to St Swithin's where he is enrolled as Junior Casualty House Surgeon. However, some rather unfortunate incidents with Mr Justice Hopwood, as well as one of his patients inexplicably coughing up nuts and bolts, mean that promotion passes him by – and goes instead to Bingham, his odious rival. After a series of disastrous interviews, Gordon cuts his losses and visits a medical employment agency. To his disappointment, all the best jobs have already been snapped up, but he could always turn to general practice...

## Doctor Gordon's Casebook

'Well, I see no reason why anyone should expect a doctor to be on call seven days a week, twenty-four hours a day. Considering the sort of risky life your average GP leads, it's not only inhuman but simple-minded to think that a doctor could stay sober that long...'

As Dr Richard Gordon joins the ranks of such world-famous diarists as Samuel Pepys and Fanny Burney, his most intimate thoughts and confessions reveal the life of a GP to be not quite as we might expect... Hilarious, riotous and just a bit too truthful, this is Richard Gordon at his best.

# RICHARD GORDON

## GREAT MEDICAL DISASTERS

Man's activities have been tainted by disaster ever since the serpent first approached Eve in the garden. And the world of medicine is no exception. In this outrageous and strangely informative book, Richard Gordon explores some of history's more bizarre medical disasters. He creates a catalogue of mishaps including anthrax bombs on Gruinard Island, destroying mosquitoes in Panama, and Mary the cook who, in 1904, inadvertently spread Typhoid across New York State. As the Bible so rightly says, 'He that sinneth before his maker, let him fall into the hands of the physician.'

## THE PRIVATE LIFE OF JACK THE RIPPER

In this remarkably shrewd and witty novel, Victorian London is brought to life with a compelling authority. Richard Gordon wonderfully conveys the boisterous, often lusty panorama of life for the very poor – hard, menial work; violence; prostitution; disease. *The Private Life of Jack The Ripper* is a masterly evocation of the practice of medicine in 1888 – the year of Jack the Ripper. It is also a dark and disturbing medical mystery. Why were his victims so silent? And why was there so little blood?

'…horribly entertaining…excitement and suspense buttressed with authentic period atmosphere' – *The Daily Telegraph*

## TITLES BY RICHARD GORDON AVAILABLE DIRECT FROM HOUSE OF STRATUS

| Quantity | | £ | $(US) | $(CAN) | € |
|---|---|---|---|---|---|
| | THE CAPTAIN'S TABLE | 6.99 | 11.50 | 15.99 | 11.50 |
| | DOCTOR AND SON | 6.99 | 11.50 | 15.99 | 11.50 |
| | DOCTOR AT LARGE | 6.99 | 11.50 | 15.99 | 11.50 |
| | DOCTOR AT SEA | 6.99 | 11.50 | 15.99 | 11.50 |
| | DOCTOR IN CLOVER | 6.99 | 11.50 | 15.99 | 11.50 |
| | DOCTOR IN LOVE | 6.99 | 11.50 | 15.99 | 11.50 |
| | DOCTOR IN THE HOUSE | 6.99 | 11.50 | 15.99 | 11.50 |
| | DOCTOR IN THE NEST | 6.99 | 11.50 | 15.99 | 11.50 |
| | DOCTOR IN THE NUDE | 6.99 | 11.50 | 15.99 | 11.50 |
| | DOCTOR IN THE SOUP | 6.99 | 11.50 | 15.99 | 11.50 |
| | DOCTOR IN THE SWIM | 6.99 | 11.50 | 15.99 | 11.50 |
| | DOCTOR ON THE BALL | 6.99 | 11.50 | 15.99 | 11.50 |
| | DOCTOR ON THE BOIL | 6.99 | 11.50 | 15.99 | 11.50 |
| | DOCTOR ON THE BRAIN | 6.99 | 11.50 | 15.99 | 11.50 |
| | DOCTOR ON TOAST | 6.99 | 11.50 | 15.99 | 11.50 |
| | DOCTOR'S DAUGHTERS | 6.99 | 11.50 | 15.99 | 11.50 |
| | DR GORDON'S CASEBOOK | 6.99 | 11.50 | 15.99 | 11.50 |
| | THE FACEMAKER | 6.99 | 11.50 | 15.99 | 11.50 |
| | GOOD NEIGHBOURS | 6.99 | 11.50 | 15.99 | 11.50 |

ALL HOUSE OF STRATUS BOOKS ARE AVAILABLE FROM GOOD BOOKSHOPS OR
DIRECT FROM THE PUBLISHER:

Internet: **www.houseofstratus.com** including author interviews, reviews, features.

Email: **sales@houseofstratus.com** please quote author, title and credit card details.

## TITLES BY RICHARD GORDON AVAILABLE DIRECT
## FROM HOUSE OF STRATUS

| Quantity | £ | $(US) | $(CAN) | € |
|---|---|---|---|---|
| GREAT MEDICAL DISASTERS | 6.99 | 11.50 | 15.99 | 11.50 |
| GREAT MEDICAL MYSTERIES | 6.99 | 11.50 | 15.99 | 11.50 |
| HAPPY FAMILIES | 6.99 | 11.50 | 15.99 | 11.50 |
| INVISIBLE VICTORY | 6.99 | 11.50 | 15.99 | 11.50 |
| LOVE AND SIR LANCELOT | 6.99 | 11.50 | 15.99 | 11.50 |
| NUTS IN MAY | 6.99 | 11.50 | 15.99 | 11.50 |
| THE SUMMER OF SIR LANCELOT | 6.99 | 11.50 | 15.99 | 11.50 |
| SURGEON AT ARMS | 6.99 | 11.50 | 15.99 | 11.50 |
| THE PRIVATE LIFE OF DR CRIPPEN | 6.99 | 11.50 | 15.99 | 11.50 |
| THE PRIVATE LIFE OF FLORENCE NIGHTINGALE | 6.99 | 11.50 | 15.99 | 11.50 |
| THE PRIVATE LIFE OF JACK THE RIPPER | 6.99 | 11.50 | 15.99 | 11.50 |

ALL HOUSE OF STRATUS BOOKS ARE AVAILABLE FROM GOOD BOOKSHOPS OR
DIRECT FROM THE PUBLISHER:

**Hotline:** UK ONLY: 0800 169 1780, please quote author, title and credit card details.
INTERNATIONAL: +44 (0) 20 7494 6400, please quote author, title and
credit card details.

**Send to:** House of Stratus Sales Department
24c Old Burlington Street
London
W1X 1RL
UK

WLB
333
28/05/2003

Please allow for postage costs charged per order plus an amount per book as set out in the tables below:

|  | £(Sterling) | $(US) | $(CAN) | €(Euros) |
|---|---|---|---|---|
| **Cost per order** | | | | |
| UK | 2.00 | 3.00 | 4.50 | 3.30 |
| Europe | 3.00 | 4.50 | 6.75 | 5.00 |
| North America | 3.00 | 4.50 | 6.75 | 5.00 |
| Rest of World | 3.00 | 4.50 | 6.75 | 5.00 |
| **Additional cost per book** | | | | |
| UK | 0.50 | 0.75 | 1.15 | 0.85 |
| Europe | 1.00 | 1.50 | 2.30 | 1.70 |
| North America | 2.00 | 3.00 | 4.60 | 3.40 |
| Rest of World | 2.50 | 3.75 | 5.75 | 4.25 |

PLEASE SEND CHEQUE, POSTAL ORDER (STERLING ONLY), EUROCHEQUE, OR INTERNATIONAL MONEY ORDER (PLEASE CIRCLE METHOD OF PAYMENT YOU WISH TO USE)
MAKE PAYABLE TO: STRATUS HOLDINGS plc

Cost of book(s): —————————— Example: 3 x books at £6.99 each: £20.97
Cost of order: —————————— Example: £2.00 (Delivery to UK address)
Additional cost per book: ————— Example: 3 x £0.50: £1.50
Order total including postage: ———— Example: £24.47

Please tick currency you wish to use and add total amount of order:

☐ £ (Sterling)    ☐ $ (US)    ☐ $ (CAN)    ☐ € (EUROS)

VISA, MASTERCARD, SWITCH, AMEX, SOLO, JCB:

☐☐☐☐☐☐☐☐☐☐☐☐☐☐☐☐☐☐☐☐

**Issue number (Switch only):**

☐☐☐

**Start Date:**                    **Expiry Date:**

☐☐/☐☐                      ☐☐/☐☐

**Signature:** ——————————————

**NAME:** ————————————————————

**ADDRESS:** ————————————————————

————————————————————

**POSTCODE:** ——————————

Please allow 28 days for delivery.

Prices subject to change without notice.
Please tick box if you do not wish to receive any additional information. ☐

House of Stratus publishes many other titles in this genre; please check our website (**www.houseofstratus.com**) for more details.